THE RED CAPE SOCIETY, BOOK 6

MELANIE KARSAK

CLOCKPUNK PRESS

Lycans and Legends
A Red Riding Hood Retelling
The Red Cape Society, Book 6
Copyright © 2019 Clockpunk Press
All rights reserved. No part of this book may be used or reproduced without permission from the author.
This is a work of fiction. References to historical people, organizations, events, places, and establishments are the product of the author's imagination or are used fictitiously. Any resemblance to living persons is purely coincidental.
Editing by Becky Stephens Editing
Proofreading by Contagious Edits
Cover art by Art by Karri

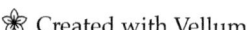 Created with Vellum

Novel Description

SOMEONE IS TRYING TO ASSASSINATE THE QUEEN

After foiling an assassination attempt on Queen Victoria, Clemeny is on the hunt. Who is after the queen? To find answers, Clemeny Louvel must travel to the one place she's been avoiding, the Summer Country.

Hiding amongst the mist and standing stones are secrets about Clemeny's case—and her past. An ancient grudge with roots deep in the heart of Britannia is about to unfold on the Victorian stage. Unless Clemeny can stop it first.

Dive into the exciting final chapter of Clemeny's adventures in *Lycans and Legends*, a retelling of the classic Red

Riding Hood fairy tale by *New York Times* bestselling author Melanie Karsak.

For Erhan

Lycans and Legends

CHAPTER 1
Isadora

S itting in the sunny parlor of the Briarwood home, I watched the flurry of activity around me with equal amounts of excitement and heart-stopping paralysis. Jessica attempted to soothe the squalling baby lying in the cradle. Quinn, who was as pale as milk, spun in circles.

"A bowl of fresh water and a towel," Jessica told Quinn patiently—for the third time.

"But she's bleeding," Quinn said, a tone of panic in his voice the likes of which I'd only ever heard when Fenton's entire pack was chasing us down an alley.

"No need to worry, dear Quinlan. It's just a little scratch. She needs her fingernails trimmed, that's all," Renee, Jessica's cousin who'd come to help with the baby, told him.

Quinn quickly poured some water, shooting me a frantic glance as he did so. "Clem, do something."

"Like what, *Quinlan*?"

In the bassinet, Baby Briarwood lay crying, a bleeding red scratch across her cheek. Poor, tiny thing. I knew well enough that a scratch on the face hurt like a bugger.

I rose, snatched a pile of clean towels, then followed Quinn.

Chuckling, Jessica took the bowl of water from Quinn and set it aside. She then turned to me, taking the towels. "You two. Seriously? After everything you have seen? It's just a little scratch. Clem, take Quinn outside for some air."

I didn't protest. Quinn's panic was making me feel panicked.

"But Isadora," Quinn protested, staring down at the baby who kicked her legs with such fervor that it looked like she wanted to run away from all the commotion but couldn't get traction. She squirmed with annoyance and frustration. Big tears rolled down her cheeks.

Renee dipped one of the towels in some water then gently wiped the blood away from the baby's cheek.

"She'll be all right," Jessica reassured him. "We'll clean the scratch, get her nails trimmed, and everything will be fine."

I bent over the cradle. Little Isadora Briarwood

really was beautiful. With a mop of dark hair that curled around her ears and bright blue eyes, she was a ball of perfection.

A ball of screaming, red-faced perfection.

Jessica set her hand on my shoulder.

When I met her glance, she tilted her head toward the front door.

"Goodbye, Isadora. I'll be back again soon," I told her.

She cried in reply, her bottom lip trembling.

"Right, then. Come on, Quinn. I want to show you something," I said, motioning for the nervous father to follow me.

Jessica patted my arm, then Quinn and I headed toward the front of the house. I couldn't help but notice that both of us had a little extra spring in our steps. Snatching my red cape, I pulled it on then headed out, Quinn following behind me.

London's fiercest werewolf hunters running from a five-month-old baby. What a fine sight.

"Wow, you weren't kidding," Quinn said as he approached the steamauto sitting on the Twickenham street just outside his house. The gorgeous machine, all chrome, metal, and silver paint shimmered in the morning sunlight. "Doesn't it bother your stomach?"

"A bit. Harper drives it more than I do."

"Hmm," Quinn mused as he ran his finger along the

fender of the machine. "A gift from the Cabells, you said?"

I nodded.

"Where is Harper?"

"Working. Her Majesty is attending the opening of the Boatswain museum this afternoon. Edwin has Harper busy with advance detail."

"Her Majesty should stay in Buckingham. What in the hell is she thinking of making a public appearance?"

"I guess she's trying to show she's not afraid."

Over the last two months, there had been two attempts on Her Majesty's life. At first, the matter was handled by the Queen's non-preternatural wing of intelligence operatives. But as details unfolded, the Red Capes were drawn in. Someone—or some*thing*—was gunning for Her Majesty. It wouldn't be the first time a preternatural tried to take out a monarch.

"Do they have any leads yet?"

"Edwin's been handling the case. I haven't been let in on the details."

Because I broke it off with him. Now that we weren't together, Edwin didn't tell me anything I didn't need to know. In fact, Edwin hardly told me anything at all. I never saw him.

"Well, I suppose that makes sense. If it's not a werewolf issue…" Quinn said with a shrug. He lifted the bonnet on the auto to have a look.

"I've been occupied anyway," I said, sounding far more dismissive than I felt. I really didn't like the idea that someone was after Victoria, and I didn't know who or why. I hadn't been assigned to the case, but I'd already had my feelers out. Surely someone in the Dark District would know what was going on.

"Occupied with what?" Quinn asked.

"What's left of the Conklin pack is misbehaving. They have a new beta, Acwellen. At best, he despises Lionheart. At worst, I think he'd like to murder the alpha. But…I don't know. Something is off. Word in the Dark District is that someone in Conklin murdered a witch. And all of the pack members have gone to ground. They're up to something. I don't know what."

"You think they're involved with the attacks on the Queen?" Quinn asked.

"I'm not sure."

"And what do Little Red's instincts tell her?" Quinn asked with a grin.

"That they know something."

Quinn nodded. "Agreed. Have you told Edwin?"

"No. Not until I know for sure. Besides, Edwin is busy."

"Is that so?" Quinn asked, raising an eyebrow at me.

I wasn't making excuses. Edwin was busy. In fact, he was so busy that I almost never saw him, a fact about which I was extremely grateful. "Yes."

Naturally, things had been awkward since I'd broken off with Edwin. I'd gone back to strictly working the night shift, only stopping by headquarters when absolutely necessary—which was usually in the middle of the night when Edwin was most definitely not going to be there. Any new cases we'd been asked to track down had been given to Harper, who didn't have to hide from our boss.

"Funny how both you and Edwin are so preoccupied. Why is Edwin so *busy*?" Quinn asked.

"Well, aside from the fact that—potentially—a preternatural is trying to murder the Queen, there was an incident in India. A number of field agents were killed. Artifacts and Archives were involved."

"Artifacts and Archives... Is Greystock all right?" Quinn asked as he closed the bonnet. Rounding the side of the auto, he slipped into the driver's seat.

I got in on the passenger side.

"Bloody chilly for spring," I grumbled as I slammed the door shut. "Greystock is fine. She was in Ireland when the incident happened. Whatever happened has that whole division scurrying. No one is sharing details."

Quinn nodded thoughtfully as he gripped the wheel of the auto. "So you have werewolves up to their usual nonsense, a preternatural trying to take out Her Majesty, a mess involving Artifacts and Archives in a field outpost in India, and no one is talking. Sounds like a storm is brewing."

"That it does."

"So explain to me again why Her Majesty is attending a museum opening?"

"I'm guessing the name Boatswain is the reason. Rude Mechanicals business. By the by, I should get going. Harper asked me to work the opening, just in case."

Quinn huffed. "I don't like it. You need to be careful, partner."

"I will."

Quinn stroked his beard. "Well, at least I know Lionheart is keeping tabs on you. And how is Sir Richard?"

Breaking the news to Quinn that I'd thrown over Edwin for Lionheart had not been easy. I knew Quinn didn't entirely agree with my choice. I hoped he'd come around, in time. "Quinn, I..."

Quinn patted me on the shoulder. "I only want you to be happy, Clem. I really do. But poor Grand-mère."

"She took it worse than Edwin, I think. I suspect it was more the idea of losing Willowbrook Park than Edwin that actually bothered her."

He laughed. "Just be careful, partner. Lionheart has stayed alive this long for a reason."

"I trust Richard."

Quinn nodded slowly. "I should go back inside."

"I'll be back to see my Izzy again."

"Izzy?"

"Izzy. Short for Isadora, right? She looks like an Izzy."

"If you say so, Auntie Clem."

I chuckled.

Quinn opened the door and got out.

I slid into the driver's seat.

Quinn hung on my door a moment longer. "Watch your back. This jumble of a mess stinks. God knows what *they* are up to now," he said then closed the auto door.

I waved to him.

Quinn walked to the door of his house, giving me one last wave before heading inside. Pulling a lever, I activated the engine of the auto then pulled out onto the Twickenham street. As I drove off, I mulled over the details of the case once more. Quinn was right. Something was wrong here. I only hoped I figured out what it was before it was too late.

CHAPTER 2

The Boatswain Museum of Mechanicals, Clockwork, and Aether Aviation

I left Twickenham, arriving at Hungerford Market just before ten o'clock. The new museum, funded by the London Tinker's Society, was located a block away from the ever-busy marketplace. It seemed like all of London had turned out to celebrate the opening. Of course, Londoners didn't care much about the obscure tinkers, clockmakers, or engineers whose works would be on display in the new museum. It was the Hall of Aviation that had brought out the crowd. More passionate about aether sports than rugby or football, it was the airships that drew people in. Brits loved airship racing.

I pushed through the crowd, stopping in the edibles aisle to grab a scone. I was late, but how could I resist the allure of butter and sugar? Nibbling my clove-and-orange pastry, I made my way to the museum.

A platform had been set up at the base of the stairs leading into the museum. The crowd assembled behind wrought-iron security barriers placed between them and the stage. The perimeter was guarded by the Bow Street Runners. Some palace guards had already arrived and were in position on the platform.

I eyed the setup.

The stage was secure. It was a lot of security. Everywhere I looked, I saw uniforms. Victoria didn't usually travel with so much detail.

I flashed the badge on my vest to the constable then headed up the steps toward the museum. Agent Fox was at the door.

"Martin," I said, giving him a nod.

"You're late, Louvel," he said with a grin.

"No, I'm not. Want a bite of scone?"

He shook his head. "No, thanks," he said with a laugh. "Hunter and Agent Harper are inside."

The wind whipped up the steps and under my cloak. I shuddered. "Bloody cold for March, isn't it? Shouldn't it be warming up by now?"

"Better get used to it."

"And that's because?"

"Since you were late—of course, you're not late, right?—you missed the briefing. You've been assigned a spot on the platform with Her Majesty. In the cold. In front of the crowd."

"Oh, no. They did not."

"Oh, yes. They did. I guess that's what you get for *not* being late."

I chuckled then turned and headed inside.

"Hope the scone was worth it," Agent Fox called. I could hear the smile in his voice.

I took another bite. The scone was good, but it was not worth getting stationed in front of the crowd. I touched the scar under my eye. It wasn't *that* visible anymore, but still.

I gazed up at the front of the museum. It really was an extraordinary structure. A massive clock trimmed the entrance above the door. The gears, exposed behind glass, turned and clicked. The moving cogs also powered a carousel of armored soldiers just outside the door. Like the figures on a cuckoo clock, they rotated, each figure taking a turn to face the crowd. The clockwork soldiers, dressed in an array of armor from different time periods, saluted the crowd when it came to the front. The massive structure looked like a living clock.

I headed inside.

Suspended from the ceiling above the main foyer was a massive planetary orrery. The planets, situated on metal arms, slowly circled around the sun, the constellations moving on metal bands. It was an impressive sight. Also on display in the main lobby was an antique airship. The burner on the balloon of the old, one-person craft had been lit. The ship was aloft several feet off the ground but was tethered down by ropes. The airship swayed. It was an extraordinary work of aviation history—if one liked that sort of thing.

Glancing around the room, I spotted a number of Bow Street Runners, palace guards, and other secret service officers in their tell-tale black suits. But on the balconies of the upper levels of the museum, I saw red capes.

Why had Victoria asked for us to be there? What was going on? How was this related to the India case? I suddenly felt very annoyed. Whatever was happening, it was being kept from us field agents. Edwin had pulled Harper in for the task to help him with detail, which was fine. Harper had taken over all the communication between Edwin and me ever since All Hallows. It had seemed easier just to avoid one another and let Harper be the intermediary. It worked. Edwin and I never saw one another. I could avoid feeling like the worst human being on the face of the planet, and Edwin could avoid heartbreak. But the side effect was that I didn't know what was going on beyond my beat. Now everything was just...murky.

"Clemeny," Harper called.

I looked up to see Harper, Hank, Cressida, Pippa, and Edwin at the entrance of the Aviation exhibit. Harper waved for me to join them.

Edwin looked up when he heard Harper call my name.

My stomach clenched when our gazes met.

I smiled lightly.

Edwin returned the gesture—briefly—then looked away.

I swallowed hard, stuffed the last bite of scone into my pocket for safekeeping, then joined them.

Harper was pointing to her clipboard. As I approached, Edwin stepped closer to her, suddenly taking an intense interest in the papers thereon.

"You're late," Harper scolded me.

"No. You said ten."

"Exactly. It's ten-thirty," Harper said.

"Your clock is wrong," I replied.

Harper pointed to the massive clock that made up the entire wall behind me. "Why don't you tell that to the London Clockmakers Society?" she said with a shake of the head, but I also saw her grin.

"The auto gave me some trouble. And it's a bit of a drive from Twickenham."

"So it has nothing to do with those crumbs on your shirt?" Harper retorted.

The others chuckled.

"Did you at least bring us something to eat?" Hank asked.

"Sorry."

"Figures," Harper said with a light laugh. She then turned to Edwin. "Okay, Edwin, as I was saying..."

When did she start calling him Edwin?

"Agents are stationed throughout the museum," she said, tapping her finger on the clipboard. "These sections of the museum are closed. I reassigned museum security, placing them at the entrances and exits. Her Majesty plans to visit the aviation wing, following this path, after the opening. She'll depart thereafter, leaving through this exit. I have agents stationed all along here," she said, pointing once more.

Edwin laced his hands behind his back as he studied the clipboard. "Yes. Very good," he said, but then he began rocking onto his heels.

"The guards in the aviation wing have all been verified and searched, as you requested. Everyone is in place who should be there," Harper said.

"Well done," Edwin told her.

"And how is Her Majesty arriving?" I asked.

"By airship," Edwin answered, but he didn't meet my eye.

"She'll be very exposed climbing down a ladder," I said.

"They've made a special basket to lower her more

fashionably—and quickly," Edwin explained, still not looking at me.

"Are any agency airships accompanying her?" I asked.

"Two. They'll fly in with her from Buckingham," Harper replied.

I nodded. Avoiding Edwin had left me out of the loop, a fact that didn't sit well with me. I was good at my job, partially because I wanted to be the best agent in the Red Capes. One day, I hoped I would be promoted. Only the best agents were tasked with events like this. I would have thought, after the incident with Marlowe, and Krampus, and the Vikings, and all the rest, that Her Majesty had noticed my work. Apparently, I had over-estimated my successes at the agency. With Edwin at the helm, and Edwin and me in the most awkward situation ever, things weren't looking good for my career. I never thought I should be worried about my job, but it was Harper leading this detail, not me.

I cast a sidelong glance at Edwin. His jaw was clenched, and he was tapping his fingers behind his back.

Something wasn't right here.

Was that something me?

"Hank and I will sweep the Aviation Hall one more time then get into position," Cressida said.

"I'll check out front," Pippa added.

Edwin nodded to them, and the other agents left.

"Agent Fox spoiled your surprise. I understand I'm on duty outside," I said, giving Harper a knowing look.

"I wasn't the one—" Harper began.

"Her Majesty asked for you," Edwin interrupted.

Steeling myself, I met his eyes. It hurt to be this close to him. It bothered me to know I had wounded Edwin. I cared about him. I really did. It was just... "Why?" I asked.

Edwin cleared his throat, then cleared it again. "She said she wants her best agents close by. You and Harper—and me—we'll all be on the platform with her."

"All right," I said cautiously. "You do know it's cold out there," I said with a slight grin, trying to ease the tension.

Harper smiled. "We'll only be out there for a few minutes. There will be general introductions by the London Tinker's Society, then Archibald Boatswain is scheduled to speak. Afterward, Her Majesty will open the museum, then we'll all come back inside."

"Archibald Boatswain?" I asked.

"Archibald Boatswain IV," Harper clarified.

I nodded then scanned around once more. "There is a lot of security—well done, Harper—but maybe Her Majesty should have declined the invitation to come, all things considered. Do we have any leads on her would-be assassin?" I asked Edwin.

"We're still sorting out the details," he said then cleared his throat again.

He was lying.

I cast a glance at Harper.

She was also eyeing Edwin, an odd expression on her face.

"All right. Let's say I buy that for the moment—which I do not—do we know what kind of preternatural we're keeping an eye out for? In my case, quite literally."

Edwin laughed softly then shook his head. "I should have known. No. We don't. That is why we have our best eyes on the ground."

"And if you're upset about having to stand outside in the cold, you should know it could be worse. Agent Rose is *under* the museum," Harper said.

"Oh, she must be pleased about that," I said with a smirk. Knowing Agent Rose was lurking around had the dual effect of setting me on edge and putting me at ease. In a fight, Rose was handy to have around. But the fact that she'd been invited was proof enough that all was not well.

"I'll wander about for a few minutes, see if I notice anything. It would be helpful if I knew what I was looking for," I told Edwin.

He didn't say anything.

"Right."

"You need to be outside and on the podium by eleven fifteen. No later," Harper told me, a stern look on her face.

I rolled my eyes. "Stop worrying, partner. Everything is going to be fine," I said, but there was a nagging feeling in my stomach that something wasn't right. Edwin was not telling us everything—which I hated. Well, I'd just have to figure things out on my own.

LEAVING HARPER AND EDWIN BEHIND, I HEADED BACK across the museum. There was a plaque beside the antique airship in the foyer. I was right. It was one of the original airships designed by Archibald Boatswain I. The airship was gifted to the museum from Lord Rhys and Lady Isabelle Llewellyn. How posh.

Glancing down the Hall of Clockwork, I felt a strange tug. I headed in that direction.

A museum guard stood at the end of the hall.

"Dim in there, Agent," he told me.

"Just having a glance about," I replied then went inside.

He was right. Inside the hall, the gaslamps were lit but on low. The flickering flames brought the polished wood floors and walls to life. They glowed in rich shades of amber. The dim light cast long shadows in the room. I passed through a hall entryway where rudimentary clockwork devices were on display. Pausing a moment, I eyed an exhibition of small, wind-up gnome men. The little toys stared at me with their beady glass eyes. A windup key lay in the exhibition along with them. I read the plaque on the wall:

The Scarlette Automaton.

The clockwork skeletal structure prominent in today's most advanced automatons was initially designed by Missus Scarlette Boatswain as a means to animate toys. Missus Boatswain is the first tinker to fashion a fully-functioning automaton. The Scarlette Automaton is the signature design used in the creation of automatons fashioned by the Boatswain Colossus Corporation. From gnomes to giants, today's automatons first found life through the gift of childlike wonder.

Cute.

And a little creepy.

The eldest gnome held out a silk rose that looked as though he was offering it to me. Had he been holding that before? I couldn't remember. I squinted at the creatures with my mooneye. Childlike wonder. Hmm. Something about these little buggers was off. But they were tiny, clockwork gnomes. In a glass display. Not a threat.

Passing down the narrow corridor, I emerged into an elaborate chamber filled with amazing clockwork devices. Steamcycles, velocipedes, steamautos, automatons of every shape, size, and use filled the room. The walls themselves were made of gears and cogs that turned and clanged.

Now, this was something.

This was the future.

My palms itched.

Of course.

Of course, they did.

"So, who is in here?" I whispered.

Exhaling slowly and deeply, I narrowed my vision and scanned the place. Automatons always triggered my senses. It was something about the way they were made. I knew they were no more than cogs, gears, and ethics boards, but something about them always set me on edge.

"Any sign of demons?" a voice called from behind me.

I turned to find Edwin.

My stomach tightened. "No, thank god."

He had to bring up our first date.

"Anything?" Edwin asked, looking around the room.

"I'm not sure, but it wouldn't be a bad idea to have someone stationed here. Just in case." I looked back at Edwin.

He was staring at me. "All right."

I swallowed hard. "Edwin…how have you been?"

He exhaled softly. "Well. I mean, I'm well. And you? How are you?"

"I'm all right. Edwin…I just…I don't know what to say."

"You don't have to say anything."

"I know, but I hate that it's like this between us now."

Edwin smiled softly, but I saw the strain on his face. "Yes. Me too. I don't…I'm not angry or sad. At least, not anymore. I have…perspective. I only want what's best for you. Even if that isn't me. I only want what's best for both of us, actually. Maybe…maybe we should talk sometime."

I nodded. "All right. Sure. Edwin—"

"I'll go ensure we have some extra guards in here. Let us know if you see anything," he said then turned to go.

I stepped toward him but stopped. No. I shouldn't say more. *I* had let *him* go. He had hurt me at the All Hallows Ball, allowing his godmother to treat me like I was rubbish, but that wasn't why I had ended it. *I* had let *him* go. I had let him go…for Lionheart. Now, I needed to give Edwin space. I owed him that.

I listened to his footsteps as he walked away.

Closing my eyes, I tried to master the emotions that tugged at me. This was not the time to get sentimental. I had a job to do. Trying to refocus, I scanned the room once more. Whatever I had felt there, I didn't sense it now. Maybe it had been Edwin. Perhaps he had triggered my senses. That seemed logical. Now the only thing I was sensing was the clockwork gnomes. Not helpful. I gave the room one last look. Why in the world did automatons unnerve me so? Strange. They were just metal, right?

Turning, I left the hall.

When I passed by the gnomes, I eyed the little elder of the group once more. This time, he was holding out a needle. There was nothing menacing about his posture. It was more like he was trying to be helpful.

I tapped on the glass. "Sorry, chap. But if something is on its way, I'm afraid that won't be much help. Thanks for the offer, though. And by the by, you and your little troupe, whatever you are, need to stay out of mischief. Got it?" I said then turned and walked away.

Great, now I was talking to garden gnomes.

CHAPTER 3
Her Royal Baitness

The wind whipped down the London street as the massive crowd assembled for the opening. On stage were a number of members of the London Tinker's Society, Harper, Edwin, and a handsome, middle-aged gentleman with curly brown hair and startling green eyes who identified himself as Archibald Boatswain IV, and me. We all waited patiently, eyes on the sky, for Her Majesty.

I inhaled slowly and let my gaze dance across the group assembled there. I hated having all these eyes on me. It worked my nerves. But there was this strange buzzing in my ears. It wasn't really a sound; just a feeling. My senses were on edge. There was no reason to think anything was going to happen. All of this was just precaution, right? Edwin was just making sure that Victoria was safe.

I looked back at the people assembled on the platform. This time, I noticed that a vast majority of the men and women seated there, members of the London Tinker's Society, were also wearing nondescript lapel pens with the initials R.M. encapsulated in a circle.

The Rude Mechanicals were here.

Why?

My gaze slid across the esteemed but secret group. They looked...nervous.

Surely, they wouldn't hold such a public event if they were expecting something.

Unless.

Unless, quite the opposite. Would they hold such an event because they *were* expecting something to happen?

Hell's bells.

Was Victoria acting as bait?

Bait for what?

I glanced at Edwin.

Apparently, my expression said everything.

He nodded.

Dammit, dammit, dammit.

They were trying to smoke out someone or something. Whose stupid idea was this? And why hadn't anyone told me? No wonder they wanted me on the podium. I was the only goddamned early warning system they had.

I turned to the museum. The clock overhead ticked loudly. I could hear it over the murmuring of the crowd. I closed my eyes and tried to feel. Something. Anything.

The wind blew my hood back, pulling my long, black hair out of the back of my cape. The palms of my hands tingled.

Clemeny…Clemeny Louvel.

I looked back at Edwin and nodded.

He tensed his jaw. The story behind the opening, the extra security, all of it, was slowly beginning to reveal itself. This was all a smokescreen for something larger taking place. But what?

I stared at Harper with such intensity that she turned and looked. Her brow was furrowed, her face all scrunched up, as if she, too, were beginning to put some pieces together. I watched her face clear as the puzzle came together for her as well. She blinked.

"Shite," she said in a whisper.

Okay, at least this wasn't Harper's idea.

"There she is. Look, there is her balloon," someone in the audience yelled.

The crowd murmured excitedly.

The illustrious members of the society waiting on the podium stood and turned, eyes lifted to the heavens, as we watched Her Majesty's airship slowly lower toward the museum.

Clemeny…Clemeny Louvel.

He's coming.

CHAPTER 4
Unmasked Bandits

The bottom of the airship opened. Two guards in matching red uniforms slid down ropes hanging from the gear galley. A moment later, a small basket descended from the belly of the airship. Inside were Her Majesty and two additional guards. They were lowering her basket down to the museum steps.

She didn't have far to go before she made it to the ground, but the ringing in my ears told me we were already too late.

I pulled my pistol and motioned to Harper. Both of us rushed to join the Queen.

Edwin, looking confused, hurried behind us.

A moment later, there was a massive crashing sound inside the museum.

A hush fell over the crowd.

Victoria's balloon basket touched down, and the Queen quickly exited as everyone turned and looked back at the museum.

A moment later, the massive doors of the museum exploded in a shower of shards and metal as an automaton busted through. The giant mech, its eyes glowing yellow, turned and tromped in the direction of Her Majesty.

I didn't have time to get distracted by the fact that the palms of my hands were tingly, that my hair was practically standing on edge, or the little voices I always heard were whispering to me. A machine was moving with deadly intent toward my Queen. And someone had to stop it.

The Bow Street Runners blew their whistles and began shouting over the panicked screaming of the crowd.

Victoria's guards rushed to her. Two of them tried to direct her back toward the airship basket. The others coaxed her toward the platform, away from the lumbering hunk of metal headed her way.

Victoria scanned all around her, a look of frustration in her eyes. Her gaze met mine. She moved toward me.

"Not good," Harper said, catching up with me. "Not good at all. You knew?"

"No. Well, not until it was too late," I said as I raced toward Her Majesty.

I heard the sound of footsteps catching up with us as Edwin and Archibald Boatswain IV ran behind us.

"Whose brilliant idea was it to use Victoria as bait?" I called to Edwin.

He frowned. "Mine."

"You, sir," I said, calling to Master Boatswain. "Go back with the other Rude Mechanicals." The illustrious group who'd been on the podium were being quickly ushered away by Hank and Cressida.

"You're going to need my help, Agent. That automaton is a Scarlette-1000 model. It's fully equipped to—" he began, but Master Boatswain's words were cut short when the machine hurled something at the Queen's airship. A moment later, there was an explosion. Her Majesty's airship went up in flames.

"Hell's bells," I said, picking up the pace as I ran to Her Majesty.

"Agent Louvel," Victoria called to me.

"Your Majesty, this way," I said, motioning to her.

Frowning, Victoria glared at the automaton then looked back at Edwin. "Well, you were right."

"Yes. But we didn't expect *that*," Edwin replied.

"There's a driver in the machine. That's the only way it can function. There's someone operating it," Master Boatswain said.

I stared at the automaton. There *was* someone—or some*thing*—inside.

"Edwin," I said, giving him a knowing glance.

"I'll go with Master Boatswain and stop the automaton. You and Harper get Her Majesty out of here," Edwin told me.

"Would be helpful if I knew what was trying to kill her," I said in a singsong.

"If we knew that, Agent Louvel, I wouldn't be here," Queen Victoria replied pertly. "Where do we go?"

"Tram under Tinker's Hall?" Harper suggested.

I eyed the massive crowd that was running screaming toward Hungerford Market.

"No. The auto," I said, tilting my chin in the direction toward which I'd left the steamauto. "That way."

"Right. Come on," Harper said then motioned to Victoria's guards to follow.

As we rushed away from the scene, I looked back. The Red Capes who had been stationed inside the museum flooded out to help Edwin and Master Boatswain with the automaton which was still ambling toward us.

"This way," I said, pointing down a dead-end alley.

"What?" Victoria protested. "Louvel, there is no exit."

"The streets will be flooded. We need to go up," I said, motioning to a ladder on the side of the building.

"Hurry, Your Majesty," one of the guards said.

Harper raced ahead and pulled down the ladder.

She nodded to me then turned and headed up, one of the guards following behind her.

"Will you be all right?" I asked Her Majesty who was wearing a dress so bulky it could have served as bedding.

"Dammit," the Queen muttered then stopped. Yanking at the jeweled sash on her waist, she unfastened the skirt of the gown then unceremoniously tossed it aside. A moment later, Her Majesty stood before me in leather trousers. The sight was so shocking and scandalous, I paused. "Not a word out of you, Louvel," she said then turned and followed the others up the ladder.

Behind us, I heard another explosion and the sound of screams. Whatever was chasing us, it was getting closer.

Victoria's guard hurried up the ladder behind her. I followed them.

As I rushed to the top, the bottom of my feet started to itch, my hands feeling shaky and odd. A wave of nausea swept over me.

I hoisted myself up and onto the roof where the others waited.

"Which way?" Harper asked.

"There," I said, pointing, but my stomach quaked. I looked back over the ledge of the building.

On the ground below, I saw a figured dressed in all

black, his features covered by a hood. He glanced upward. I couldn't see his face clearly, but I saw a glimmer of bluish-silver in his eyes.

"What the hell?" I whispered. The creature moved toward the ladder. "Harper," I called, warning in my voice. "We need to move. Now." Glancing back toward the museum, I could see the automaton. It was still heading in our direction.

Harper looked at me, reading the expression on my face.

"Right," she said. "Let's go." Harper turned and ran, the Queen and her guards following along behind her.

"Three blocks then down," I called to Harper who nodded.

We rushed across the rooftops. At least I was back on familiar ground.

Her Majesty surprised me. She was always so decadently dressed, a picture of elegance and grace, even in the face of monsters such as Krampus. But that incident taught me that my Queen was no mere posh figurehead. She had practiced old, druidic magic, sending the monster back to his own world. And now, she was hustling along behind Harper, outpacing her guards in the effort.

We dashed across the roofs, jumping the small gaps between the buildings and scrambling over the ledges.

Clemeny...Clemeny...he's coming.

I looked back to see the robed figure making his way quickly toward us.

He was fast.

Too fast.

"Hells bells. Harper, get Her Majesty out of here," I called.

Harper stopped and looked back, her eyes going from me to the figure advancing on us.

"Clemeny?" Harper called.

"Go. Just go. Get her out of here. The auto is on Market Street."

Harper frowned hard then nodded. "Your Majesty," she said, motioning for Victoria to follow her.

The Queen hesitated. She narrowed her gaze, glaring at the figure rushing toward us.

"Please, Your Majesty, go with Harper," I said then pulled my blade.

Relenting, Her Majesty and Harper turned, quickly hustling out of the way. One of her guards went with her, but another stayed behind.

"What in the hell is that?" the man asked.

"I don't know, but we're about to find out," I said then pulled my pistol. Taking aim, I shot.

The creature moved quickly, swirling around a chimney pipe. The bullet struck the bricks, causing a blast of red dust. The assailant appeared once more on the other side.

I shot again.

And again.

Each time, the figure moved fast—too fast—getting out of the way of my shots in time.

Preternatural.

"That's not possible," the guard beside me whispered, then he advanced on the figure who had caught up with us. The guard swung hard, but the would-be assassin ducked. Swiping out his leg, the assailant knocked the Queen's guard to the ground. He then pulled a dagger from his belt. The instrument had an odd blue shimmer all around it, a glow that I could only see with my mooneye.

"No," I yelled then rushed forward, knocking the man off the guard before he could land a lethal blow.

The stranger spun and leaped to his feet.

His glowing eyes scanned across the rooftop where Harper was making her escape.

Seeing the figure momentarily distracted, the guard pulled his pistol and fired. The shot took the man's attention away, and once again, the stranger moved quickly, dodging the bullet at the last moment. But his move had been clumsy. He was off balance.

Rushing forward, I kicked the assailant hard, knocking him sideways. He stumbled then fell.

Unsheathing my dagger, I rushed at him.

The figure leaped to his feet.

His hood fell back a little to reveal his long, white hair. The color of his locks was at odds with the youthful glow of his skin. But there was more. On his face were glowing blue shapes, swirling designs, like tattoos, that shimmered in the sunlight.

The man made a low, angry sound then lunged at me.

The thing about fighting werewolves is that one got used to their super-human strength. Werewolves were twice as strong, and usually twice as big, as any man. To fight a wolf, being petite was a benefit. I was small and fast. I didn't need to be strong to fight a dumb mutt like Fenton. But I did need to be quick and smart.

The problem with fighting the opponent who now stood before me was that he was also lithe, agile, and sharp-witted.

Victoria's guard, however, was not.

The guard swung at the man.

Apparently, the stranger had reached the end of his patience.

Muttering something under his breath, he turned and pushed the guard. I couldn't help but see the sparkle at the tips of the opponent's fingers, a little shimmer of blue, just before Victoria's guard tumbled over the side of the building.

The man screamed.

The stranger looked back at me, sneered, then took off in a sprint after Victoria and Harper.

"Oh, like hell you will," I said then turned and raced after him.

He was fast.

But now I was mad.

Something inside me lit up, filling me with warmth and light. There was no way in hell I was going to let this creature get past me. A warm feeling filled my stomach. It was a strange sensation, like something low and deep in the pit of my belly had awoken. I grabbed on to the feeling and used it to push myself forward.

Harper, Victoria, and the remaining guard had reached the end of the block.

I hurled myself toward the stranger, grabbing him and knocking him from his feet.

He quickly regained his footing. Jumping up, he moved to get away, but his face found my fist which was decked out in my silver knuckle-busters. I struck him. He staggered backward, then sneered, those bluish-silver eyes shimmering. Gripping his glowing blade, he advanced on me. I ducked and swept out a leg, knocking him to the ground. Grabbing my knife, I thrust.

The assailant sucked in a breath as the knife made contact. I had sliced his shoulder.

He winced.

I frowned. The silver knuckle-busters hadn't burned him—though he hadn't seemed to appreciate being whacked in the face—but my steel-and-silver blade had. This was a different kind of preternatural, something I had not seen before.

Taking the advantage, I punched him in the gut then knocked his blade from his hand.

On the street not far away, I heard the tell-tale squeal of tires.

The man spun away from me, but not before I grabbed his blade.

To my surprise, the cool metal glowed blue at my touch.

The stranger looked from the blade in my hand and back to me. He turned and listened to the sound of the escaping auto, his eyes narrowing in frustration as Harper and Victoria made their escape. There was no way he would catch them now.

He frowned hard, glaring at me, then turned and ran toward the edge of the building.

I rushed after him.

The stranger grabbed the ladder and slid down. When he reached the ground, he turned and looked up at me, glaring darkly. He then turned and rushed off upriver.

I knew where he was headed. There was a Dark

District not far away. I raced down the ladder and into the city, running after him. My lungs burned.

It seemed like I was always running.

Why didn't anything bad ever just saunter?

I caught sight of the man fleeing through the crowd as the Londoners stopped and stared. He glanced back at me.

I rushed after him.

The London streets narrowed as we neared the Dark District, a section of town dating back to the medieval period. The buildings clustered closer together, leaning toward one another at odd angles, blocking out the morning sunlight. The shops cast long shadows on the street. Gaslamps still flickered, illuminating the dim, gray space.

I stilled and tried to feel where the stranger had gone.

My instincts pulled me toward a dark, narrow alley.

I rushed in that direction in time to see the man's cloak flutter as he turned the corner at the end of the alley.

Stashing the stranger's dagger on my belt, I pulled my pistol. Ninety percent of whatever lived in the Dark District could be killed by a silver bullet, five-percent were already dead, and the rest needed a specialist. The odds were on my side.

Half-expecting the assassin to jump out at me, I turned the corner to find yet another dark alley, which I knew led to one of the uncompleted tunnels under the Thames. Aside from the success of the Brunel tunnel project farther upriver, digging tunnels under the Thames had turned out to be a terrible idea. They flooded, of course. The dark, earthen cavities were terrific places for terrible things to hide. I'd bet my good eye that was where he'd gone.

Keeping my pistol in front of me, I approached the tunnel. I scanned around me with my mooneye. There were other creatures here, dark things lingering in the alcoves and small rooms just off the entrance of the incomplete tunnel. They watched me closely.

My heart slammed in my chest.

Moving carefully, I stepped into the darkness of the tunnel.

I dug into my pocket with my free hand and pulled out the night optic goggles and slipped them on. Activating the switch, the world around me illuminated green for a moment.

Shadows moved everywhere.

I was definitely not alone.

Deep in the tunnel, a pair of glowing shining eyes looked back at me.

I raised my gun, aimed, and fired.

Hisses and whispered protests rose from the

shadows around me. Then, I saw those glimmering eyes once more.

"I own the future, Clemeny Louvel," the robed stranger called to me, his voice masculine but soft. It had a strange, menacing cadence.

A strange wind blew through the tunnel, carrying with it the dense scents of earth, loam, and smoke. It was a peculiar, putrid scent. The breeze ruffled my hair, blowing my cloak all around me.

And as suddenly as it came, the wind died.

He was gone.

CHAPTER 5
The Unthinkable

I stood staring into the void into which the stranger had disappeared. He'd opened a portal to the Otherworld here, right here, in the middle of London.

I considered his words, menacing but straightforward. If a werewolf had huffed something like that at me, I would have laughed. But something about the stranger had set me on edge. His words were not spoken like a threat. He had sounded…certain.

Lost to my thoughts, they were almost on me when I finally realized I was in danger.

Again.

"And just what are you doing so far from the light?" a deep, sultry voice asked.

For god's sakes, fangs. Really?

I sighed heavily, unable to hide my exasperation. "Hunting much more interesting prey than you."

"Hunting and failing, from what we can see. And now your heart is all a patter. We've all wondered for a long time what makes you smell so good, Clemeny Louvel. Now, we'll finally get a taste."

"Not today," a voice called from behind us.

I heard a strange sound. The sound of bullets—no, not bullets—whizzed past me. The vampires, four in all, grunted as something struck them.

I looked behind me.

Agent Rose stood there, an odd-looking crossbow in her hands.

"You might want to move, Louvel," she said, wagging a finger at the vampires.

I looked around me to see the fiends clutching stakes, which were protruding from their chests.

"Oh, damn," I said then rushed away, taking cover in an alcove close by a moment before the vampires exploded. Strange, wet, popping sounds filled the tunnel, echoing all around.

One.

Two.

Three.

Four.

When it was over, I joined Agent Rose. "And where were you all this time?" I asked, holstering my pistol.

"In the tunnels *under* the museum, thanks to Harper," she said, motioning to her boots which were covered in grime. "But all the fun was happening up top. Sorry they got in the way," she said, motioning to the heaps of what had once been vampires.

"No, not in the way, just an annoyance, like flies. I lost my mark all on my own."

She motioned toward the tunnel. "So, what was he?"

I shook my head. "I don't know." I pulled the unknown assailant's dagger from my belt. "Left this behind."

Agent Rose looked at the blade, her eyes narrowing. "It's glowing."

I nodded.

Rose extended her gloved hand and took the dagger from me. When I passed the weapon to her, the glow faded.

Rose raised an eyebrow. "Well, that's interesting. Did it glow when he had it too?"

"I...yeah. It did."

Rose weighed the weapon in her hand. She turned it over, looking at it carefully. "Not silver. Not steel, either."

I frowned. "The museum...what did you see back there? This creature wasn't working alone."

"There were boggarts. I saw one, for just a moment, before it slipped away."

"Boggarts," I said then frowned. Boggarts were dark spirits, shape-shifting creatures who never aligned themselves with anything good. For the most part, they stayed out of the way of the Red Cape Society. They worked jobs as hired men, assassins, and thieves. They were bloody hard to catch, always shifting form. The only way to catch them was to bind them in silver so they couldn't shift. "Wonderful. So we have a mystery man threatening the apocalypse, a glowing blue dagger—"

"Which only glows when you touch it."

I frowned at her.

She shrugged. "Just saying."

"—a glowing blue dagger and boggarts."

"Victoria still alive?"

"I think so. She and Harper went speeding off in my auto."

"Well, the day isn't a total loss then. I guess.

"You guess? We saved the Queen."

Agent Rose smirked to herself. "I heard."

I gave her a questioning look which she promptly ignored. "Shall we head back to headquarters before something else tries to kill us?" Agent Rose offered.

I shook my head. Whatever Rose's story was, I wasn't getting it out of her today. "Lead the way."

AGENT ROSE AND I TOOK AN UNDERGROUND TRAM BACK to headquarters. The moment we exited the lift, we could see the place in complete chaos. Everywhere I looked, agents from every division were scurrying around.

"Quite the kerfuffle," Agent Rose observed, her arms across her chest.

"Let's see if Harper is back," I said.

Not finding her at her desk, we headed toward Edwin's office. Along the way, however, we passed Agent Keung.

"He's not there," the agent told me.

"Where is he?"

"Artifacts and Archives. With Harper and Her Majesty."

"Victoria is here?" Agent Rose asked.

Keung laughed. "Couldn't you tell?" he said, motioning to the agents scurrying like rats. "A preternatural just tried to kill her, and we don't know which one. All hands on deck," he said with a chuckle then headed back to the main room.

Rose motioned to me, and we headed down a side hallway. There, we took a lift down to Artifacts and Archives.

As we went, Agent Rose studied the dagger on my belt, her pretty face scrunched up as she mulled something over.

"What is it?" I asked.

She carefully removed the dagger, studied it once more, then handed it to me.

Again, it glowed blue.

"Put on your gloves," she told me, taking the dagger.

I did as I suggested.

She returned the knife to me.

Once more, it glowed.

Frowning, she took the knife and stuck it in her own belt. "Don't touch it when we're down there. Don't let them see," she said.

I stared at her. I knew what she was implying, but I asked anyway. "Why not?"

"Do you know why it glows blue?" she asked.

"Not really. Do you?" I replied, hoping she would have some hint.

"I have a guess. Nothing specific, but don't let them see until you know why."

"Rose…" I said.

She winked at me. "Whatever it is that makes that thing glow blue, you'd better find out what it is. Soon."

The bell on the lift dinged.

Rose and I exited into the hall leading to Artifacts and Archives. Here, deep under London, a massive library and museum of curiosities were stored out of sight. We didn't get far when we heard Her Majesty's voice echoing down the hallway.

"It was all for nothing. No answers, just chaos," Her Majesty was saying.

Agent Rose and I exchanged a glance then went to the meeting room. There, Edwin, Harper, Archibald Boatswain IV, Agent Greystock, and an agent wearing Indian garb stood looking at the Queen, all of them with pained expressions on their faces.

When I entered, I caught Harper's eye.

She widened her eyes then shook her head, letting me know things were not going well.

That was obvious.

Queen Victoria looked up.

"Ah, Louvel," she said. A momentary look of relief crossed her face, but then her glance went to Agent Rose. "And Aurora Rose," she added with a half-frown. She looked away from Rose. "Well, Louvel, give me some good news."

"Good news," I said, struggling to figure out a way to spin the fact that I had lost the preternatural. "The good news is that I managed to waylay whatever preternatural was trying to murder you. I tracked him to the unfinished Brunswick tunnel at the end of the Dark District. Somehow, he opened a doorway into the Otherworld before I could arrest him."

"And she disarmed him and retrieved this," Agent Rose said, cutting in.

Rose set the dagger on the table in front of us.

Agent Greystock and the Queen went to the table to investigate. Agent Greystock picked up the weapon—it didn't glow—adjusted her spectacles, then studied it carefully. She frowned hard then handed the weapon to the Queen—it didn't glow in her grasp either.

Greystock then crossed the room and activated the intercom there.

"This is Greystock. Ask Albertus Stone to join us, please."

"Well, Eliza? Is it what we feared?" the Queen asked Agent Greystock as she looked over the dagger.

"I hesitate to say either way. Let's consult Agent Stone first."

Victoria sighed heavily then turned to the stranger. "And your division? What news?" she asked the Indian agent.

The gentleman shook his head. "Your Majesty, the artifact you inquired about is gone. And we are down five agents, including our director and his deputy."

"Wonderful. Just wonderful. Were any other artifacts taken?"

"No, Your Majesty."

"I finally get the common people in order, and now the preternatural society is imploding." She turned to

Archibald Boatswain IV. "How did a creature get into your automaton?" she snapped. But before he had a chance to answer, the Queen turned to Harper. "And how did it get past security?"

"We don't know, Your Majesty. There was no one in that hall," Harper said meekly. All the color had drained from her cheeks. I thought she might faint.

"By the time Archibald and I deactivated the automaton, the driver escaped," Edwin explained.

"It was a boggart," Agent Rose interjected.

"A boggart?" Victoria said, her voice thick with annoyance.

Agent Rose nodded. "He could have slipped into the hall in any form. Even as a mouse. No wonder he was overlooked. They are easy to miss if you don't have an eye for them. I tracked him into the Dark District but lost him there."

Edwin nodded. "A boggart. Yes, that would make sense."

"This just gets better and better," the Queen said then turned to me. "Who tried to kill me? Describe him."

"Robed. Male. Long white hair. Pale skin. Blue designs, not exactly tattoos, on his skin."

Victoria inhaled deeply and slowly, setting her fingertips on the table. "Shite," she murmured under her breath.

I raised an eyebrow at Her Majesty.

Across the room, Harper covered her mouth so she wouldn't giggle aloud.

"Here. I'm here. I'm here, Your Majesty," a rushed voice called from the hallway. A flood of footsteps approached the room. A moment later, a little man with large spectacles, an armload of papers, and an untucked shirt raced into the room. He dropped his parchments on the table then took a moment to smooth down his wild hair. "Agent Albertus Stone, Your Majesty."

Agent Greystock cleared her throat, swallowing some embarrassment. "Agent Stone is the Red Capes' best symbologist, Your Majesty."

"Oh my god," Albertus Stone said in an awed whisper when he spotted the dagger lying on the table. "Oh my god," he repeated again. Without waiting for an invitation, he lifted the dagger—it didn't glow. He pushed his spectacles onto the top of his head then dipped into his pocket. After pulling out a few miscellaneous items, tossing them carelessly onto the table, he stuck an optic into his eye. He activated the lens, which buzzed and clicked, his eye growing huge. He studied the engravings.

"Well?" Queen Victoria asked.

"Where did you get this?" Agent Stone asked.

"Irrelevant," Victoria snapped. "What is it?"

The man set the blade down then removed the optic.

He looked at the Queen. "Faerie metal. Star metal, it's sometimes called. This blade is from the Otherworld."

"And the symbols?" Agent Greystock asked.

"The symbols," Agent Stone repeated, looking at the dagger once more.

"Are they Golden Court?" the Queen asked, referring to the mostly-friendly Seelies, faeries who occasionally visited our world.

Agent Stone chuckled. "No. No. Far, far from it, Your Majesty. Oh, no. These are Unseelie symbols. These belong to the Silver Court."

"Unseelies," Edwin said, his voice thick with alarm.

Edwin was right to be upset. The Unseelies were dark faeries who hated humans at best and wanted to kill us all at worst. But the Unseelies were rarely seen in the human realm, save the brief visit by Krampus the holiday before. Before him, an Unseelie hadn't entered our world—that we knew of—for many, many years.

Queen Victoria sighed. "As we feared."

"Perhaps we should—" Edwin began, but Victoria raised a hand to stop him.

"You are dear to me, Edwin, but no more suggestions. It's not your fault, but your last idea nearly got me assassinated. No. Greystock, work with Agent Tiwari to research the artifact taken from the India division. Agent Rose," the Queen said, her voice dark. Did she dislike Agent Rose? Why? "Why don't you and your gentlemanly friend skulk about and learn which of our dark friends are throwing in allegiance with the Unseelie. You spotted the boggart. Let's see if you can spot him again."

Agent Rose nodded. "As Your Majesty commands."

Queen Victoria rolled her eyes and gave Agent Rose a sidelong glare but said nothing else. Instead, she turned and looked at me. "You disarmed the assailant, Louvel?"

"Yes, Your Majesty."

"In hand-to-hand combat?"

"Yes, Your Majesty."

"Well done. Shame that you lost him."

"I'm very sorry, Your Majesty."

"Who was he?" Archibald Boatswain IV asked.

Queen Victoria sighed. "We don't know for certain, but I have an educated and rather frightening guess," she said then turned to Edwin. "Are all of the Pellinore assets still at Willowbrook Park?"

The previous summer, Edwin, Harper, and I had assisted the Pellinore division of the Red Capes with a case that involved, of all things, a living descendant of King Arthur. We'd managed to help protect a girl named Rapunzel from a bunch of thugs who were trying to kill her and her faerie guardian, Gothel. She was the last true decedent of the ancient king. She and her interesting pets were in hiding at Edwin's family estate, Willowbrook Park, along with the Pellinore division of the Red Capes who were her sworn protectors.

"Yes," Edwin said with a nod.

"Good. I want you and Agent Harper to go to Willowbrook Park and try to connect with the faerie Gothel. Let's see if she knows anything. Louvel, rustle up Sir Richard and head to Cornwall, please."

My heart clenched. To the summer country? "Cornwall?"

"Yes. It's time our druid friends came clean. If they are still in communication with the Golden Court, then it's time to communicate," the Queen said.

"Your Majesty, what's happening?" Harper asked.

"An Unseelie tried to murder me today, Agent Harper. What we don't know yet is if he is a rogue actor or if the Silver Court is about to attempt the unthinkable."

The unthinkable. I remembered the Unseelie's words. *I own the future.* Something told me the unthinkable was about to get very real.

CHAPTER 6
Rose Petal Chocolates

After Victoria dismissed us, I motioned to Harper, and we turned to leave the room.

Agent Rose snatched the enchanted dagger off the table. "I think it would be wise if this stayed with Agent Louvel."

"But, but—" Agent Stone began in protest.

Queen Victoria raised her hand to silence him. The Queen stared at Agent Rose for a long moment. "Very well."

Rose nodded to me then we left the room.

"I didn't know Agent Hunter had a faerie stashed at Willowbrook," Agent Rose said as she fiddled with the dagger.

I nodded. "We worked a case with the Pellinores. The faerie was connected to them."

"Pellinores? Interesting. Willowbrook Park is a fine

estate. Surprised Hunter lent it to the agency," Agent Rose said as she studied the dagger once more.

"You've been there?" Agent Harper asked.

Agent Rose paused. "What? Oh. Long ago," she said then handed the dagger to me.

I took the weapon. Once again, the instrument glowed blue.

"Whoa," Harper said. "Wait. What...what is that?"

"That is an excellent question. Good luck in the summer country, Louvel," Agent Rose said with a wink. "Send the alpha my greetings."

"Clemeny," Harper whispered, looking at the blade in my hand.

"I know," I said with a shake of the head.

"Star metal," Harper said, her brow scrunching up. "Is it really faerie metal?"

"Not sure."

"Hmm," Harper mused. "Well, at least we know a couple of things."

"And that is?"

"Well, silver doesn't bother you, so that rules out about fifty percent of the supernatural types. And steel doesn't burn you either, so you aren't part faerie."

I stared at Harper.

"Look, I've been your partner long enough to know that your sixth sense coupled with that mooneye vision means something. Maybe now…maybe now you have a hint about what."

"It's a hint, but I have no idea what it means."

"Let's hope someone knows. In the meantime, I need to go to tech and grab a few things before heading out to Willowbrook. You think Gothel will talk to me?"

"If she's still there. Doubtful."

"Well, at least I'll get to see Miss Pendragon's pets again. Edwin said they've grown. A lot."

Again, Edwin. "Well, I guess you'll see."

Harper grinned, but it didn't escape my notice that she quickly dropped my gaze.

"Stay safe, partner," I told her.

She nodded. "You too."

I slipped the blade back into my belt. All right. Well then. Maybe Harper and Edwin had just grown close over the last few months because of the Cabell case. And they had worked together on the botched setup today. What a mess. Too bad no one had asked me about the plan to use Victoria as bait, which I would have solidly discouraged. But why not? Edwin had been distant. And things had been weird between us. But still. I was good at my job. Maybe it was because I'd been distracted…by wolf-shaped things.

With blond hair.

And bulging muscles.

And deep, get-lost-in eyes.

And right now, there wasn't anyone else in the world I wanted to see.

But I needed to make a stop first.

(RM)

I PULLED THE STEAMAUTO TO A STOP OUTSIDE THE STRANGE little shop on Canterbury Row at the edge of the Dark District. I slipped out and eyed the thoroughfare. Ghost orbs floated down the street away from me. And in the shadows, deep in the dark, lingered creatures trying to stay out of sight. I could feel their eyes on me. But I wasn't here for them.

I turned and headed into the shop. I was overcome at once by the musty smell, the dust making my nose itch. Everything was the same. The place was heaped with odd relics, books, and scrolls. The bone, mirror, and feather mobile over the door fluttered in the breeze.

From the back of the shop, I heard raspy whispering. Was someone else already here? Who was she talking to?

I set my hand on my knife as I made my way to the back. The Dís was sitting at her table. A single candle was lit. She was leaning in, her grungy silver hair covering her face, as she looked over a heap of bones spread out before her. She whispered in a language I didn't recognize.

"Who are you talking to?" I asked.

She paused. "The gods, Clemeny Louvel."

"Ah. The gods. How are they today?"

The Dís laughed. "The gods are always well."

"Really? One would think disbelief in their existence might put a damper on things. So, are they good listeners?"

The Dís laughed. "Loki. Loki is always listening."

"Didn't Loki fall during Ragnarok?"

"Has it been Ragnarok?"

I chuckled. "I just assumed."

The Dís laughed but didn't answer.

"I met some gods not long back," I said, settling into the seat across from her. "Nice bunch. Very…ethereal."

The Dís did not look up. She studied the bones lying on the table before her and she muttered to herself—or the gods.

I slipped the enchanted dagger from my belt and set it on the table.

At that, the Dís stopped.

"So what does Loki have to say about that?" I asked.

The ancient seer lifted her rheumy eyes and looked up at me. There was a mad, gleeful expression on her face. She swept the bones off the table and stuffed them into her pocket. She then leaned forward and looked at the dagger.

"Someone came through," she said, her voice full of wonder.

I nodded. "Do you know who?"

"Svartálfar."

I raised an eyebrow.

"Dark elf."

I nodded. We were right. It was an Unseelie. "What do they want?"

The Dís shook her head. "Nothing good. Their jealousy burns. They covet Midgard. They covet the realm of light. Danger has come, Clemeny Louvel," she said then lifted the dagger—it didn't glow. She studied the markings thereon then handed the knife to me.

I hesitated.

"Go on. Go on," she said, motioning for me to take the dagger.

When I did, the dagger lit up once more.

The Dís laughed loudly. "Maybe it is you who should be talking to the gods."

I frowned then set the blade down. "You're funnier every time I see you. Why does the blade glow when I touch it?"

The Dís lifted the dagger once more. "This is dwarven metal."

"Faerie metal."

"Dwarven metal."

"Faerie metal. Let's stop bickering. Why does it glow blue when I touch it?"

"Go to the Summer Country, Clemeny Louvel. Get your knight, and go to the Summer Country."

She wasn't going to tell me anything. Sighing, I rose. I dipped into my pocket and pulled out a packet and set it in front of her.

"What is it?" she asked excitedly.

"Dark chocolate with rose petals, pistachio, and currants."

"Rose petals," she said, scrunching up her nose in distaste.

"Don't be so closed-minded. Try it."

The Dís opened the box. Inside were dark chocolate pieces. The scent of the chocolates wafted from the box and perfumed the musty air. The Dís waggled her fingers then took out a piece and popped it into her mouth. She chewed thoughtfully.

"Not bad," she said, nodding.

"I may not know what I am. Or what you are. Or why that dagger glows blue, but one thing I do know is food."

The Dís chuckled.

I turned and headed toward the door. I was just about to exit when she called out to me.

"Can you swim, Clemeny Louvel?" the Dís asked, her mouth full of chocolate.

"Swim? Yes. Why?"

Rather than answering, the Dís simply laughed and laughed.

CHAPTER 7

Lycans

I slipped back into the auto and headed across the city to Temple Square. It was already late afternoon, the sun dipping toward the edge of the horizon. Not really the ideal time to head into pack territory, but the Templars had come to tolerate, if not accept, my presence.

I parked my auto on the street then headed to the gate.

When Sir Nash saw me approach, he checked the street then unlocked the gate.

"Good evening, Agent Louvel."

"Sir Nash."

"Lionheart will be happy to see you," he said.

I raised an eyebrow at him. "I certainly hope so."

The knight chuckled lightly. "You'll understand soon enough. He's in Middle Temple Hall."

Confused, I crossed the square to the hall. I could hear some ruckus coming from the assembly hall where the Templars met to dine and discuss pack matters. All these years, Quinn and I had watched the wolves from the rooftops, never getting too close. Now, I was in the heart of pack territory. When Quinn and I ran this town, however, Cyril and Fenton haunted the streets, that bitch Alodie causing trouble behind all our backs. Even back then, the Templars were never a problem. They were secluded, secretive, scholarly. As it turned out, the Templars were still on a mission to find the holy grail. And even now, when they ruled the realm, they had not forgotten that goal. Many of the Templars were out in the field, still on the hunt for Christ's chalice.

Given their quiet, scholarly ways, I was surprised when I heard yelling in the hall, followed by the clatter of breaking dishes.

I pulled my pistol and cautiously opened the door.

The room was long with wooden panels on the walls and a polished wood floor. The windows were lined with stained glass. At the opposite end of the room, a portrait of Richard the Lionheart towered over the space.

Not that the king's gaze had any effect on the lycan standing in the center of the room having a complete meltdown.

Jericho's eyes were glimmering red. One of his

hands was balled into a fist. The other was holding an expensive looking piece of china. The rest of the set lay in shattered pieces on the ground around him. His jaw set on edge, Jericho was staring down Lionheart like he was vying to become the new alpha.

"Clemeny," Lionheart said softly.

"Good evening. I came in to get some supper, but they told me you're fresh out of plates."

Jericho yelled in frustration then smashed the plate onto the floor. It shattered. Loudly.

I imagined Grand-mère, somewhere across town, wincing but not knowing why, her instinct to click her tongue barely in check.

"Want my silver cuffs?" I offered Lionheart.

"Hardly good parenting," Lionheart replied.

Since Jericho had come to London, Lionheart had taken the lycan under his wing. He kept the boy close to him, guiding him as best he could. I hadn't known werewolves could have the patience of a saint. But Richard never failed to surprise me.

I eyed Lionheart. He stood with his hands in the pockets and stared down the boy, but I could see he was trying to smother the bemused expression on his face.

"Jericho, I have explained to you that while your hunger may be ravenous, you will make yourself ill if you don't limit yourself. We have an unhealthy drive to consume that must be managed."

"I said I wanted *more*," Jericho screeched.

"Indeed you did. And I said no. Four plates were quite enough. Now, if you hope to eat again in the future, I suggest you stop breaking our china. It was, after all, a gift to the Templars from Queen Anne."

At that, the boy stopped. He looked at the heap at his feet. The red in his eyes dimmed a little, replaced by the rosy blush on his cheeks.

"Oh," Jericho said.

"There is a broom and dustpan in the closet. When you have finished cleaning up the mess, you may return to our chambers for some leisure reading. Do you understand?"

"Yes," the boy muttered his voice barely an octave above a growl.

"Sorry?"

"Yes, Sir Richard," Jericho said, his voice clear. He turned and looked at me, an abashed expression on his face. "Hi, Clemeny."

"Hello, my dear."

Jericho gave me a little wave then crossed the room to the broom closet.

Lionheart shook his head then joined me, motioning for us to step back outside.

"I see things are going well," I said with a grin.

"That's an improvement over how most of the day went, actually. In fact, Sir Blackwood suggested you brought Jericho to the Templars to destabilize our pack," Lionheart said with a chuckle. "In jest, of course."

"Of course. Why would I want to do that? If you're destabilized, then I can't whisk you away to come work a case with me."

"Whisk me away for a case? Ah, let me guess. This has something to do with the fireworks at the museum opening today."

"So it does. What have you heard?"

"Someone tried to assassinate the Queen—again. No wolves were involved. Other than that, merely rumors."

"Well, let me regale you. First, we had a boggart in an automaton. It smashed out of the new museum and tried to grab Her Majesty. That was a spectacle. And then there was the robed assassin. Apparently, the Rude Mechanicals suspected someone might try to come after Victoria again. Her presence at the opening was an attempt to smoke the assailant out."

"Ah," Lionheart mused. "Rather a foolish risk to put the monarch in harm's way."

"Agreed. I was unaware of the plan until the last moment."

"Indeed?"

I nodded.

"I see," Lionheart said, a guilty expression stealing

across his face. While I didn't talk about it much, I was very sure Lionheart knew that my shift in companionship from Edwin to him was bound to cause tension on my job. The look on his face told me he knew, and he was sorry.

"It's all right," I reassured him.

He nodded apologetically. "The assassin was a boggart?"

We exited Middle Hall. The sun was dipping low on the horizon, the sky illuminated in deep shades of red, gold, and pink. The wind whipped across the square.

"Agent Rose went to track him down."

Lionheart chuckled lightly. "If she finds him, god help him."

"Do you know Agent Rose well?" I asked in surprise.

"We've crossed paths in the past. Her and her companion. But the question remains, who hired the boggart?"

"Ah, now, that is the question of the day," I said then pulled the dagger from my belt and handed it to Lionheart, waiting anxiously to see what would happen when he touched it.

Lionheart stared at the dagger in my hand. "Clemeny..." he whispered.

I nodded and pressed the dagger toward him again.

He reached out and took the blade.

Nothing.

I frowned.

He lifted the instrument and studied the engravings thereon.

"Well, professor?" I asked.

He grunted, making that low wolfy sound I had come to adore. "Where did you get this?"

"I disarmed the would-be assassin."

"*You* disarmed the assassin."

"Don't sound so surprised," I chided Lionheart.

"I certainly don't disregard your prowess in battle, but do you know what this is?"

"Star metal."

Lionheart nodded. "So it is."

"We believe it was an Unseelie who went after Victoria today. Who? Why? We don't know. Which brings me back to my case. I know Conklin yelps are stirring up trouble, but do you suppose the pack would mind if I borrowed you for a few days?"

"And where are we going?"

"To talk—I hope—to the druids."

Lionheart looked at me. He knew as well as I did what a trip meant, not just for the case, but for me personally.

"Given Jericho's temperament, I believe the pack would be horrified beyond measure if I try to leave."

"Then I guess he'll have to come along."

"Oh, Clemeny. That is a terrible idea."

"Well, if you ask around, I'm sure everyone thinks you and I are full of terrible ideas. One more can't hurt. Besides, there's no danger in talking to the druids. The worst they can do is ignore us."

"Don't underestimate Celtic wizardry."

"I don't. But I have this," I said, taking the dagger from Lionheart's hand with my bare palm. At once, it began to glow. "And something tells me that the druids might be interested in why it does that."

"Clemeny," Lionheart said with a shake of the head.

I chuckled. "Are you coming or not?"

"I need to talk to Blackwood. Conklin is up to something, but I'm very sure Blackwood will be happy to take over if I promise to take Jericho with me. First thing in the morning, then?"

I nodded. "You drive. I'll leave the auto to Harper."

"Very well. *We* will see you at the grotto in the morning. Now I just need to go convince Jericho that he wants to come."

"I doubt you'll have any problem with that."

"Why is that?

"You're very persuasive," I said, stepping closer to him.

"Am I?" he replied, wrapping his arm around me and pulling me closer.

I gazed up into his eyes. My heart beat hard. "Yes," I whispered in reply, unable to form an acceptable witty comeback.

He reached out and gently stroked the scar on my face. "Look who is convincing whom," he said then set a soft kiss on my lips. The sweet and salty tastes on his tongue, the feel of his body pressed against mine, and a terrible but wonderful sense of want washed through me.

It seemed that Lionheart shared the sentiment. It was only when we heard a door open nearby that we broke apart.

Lionheart coughed lightly then adjusted his waistcoat. "Very well, Agent Louvel. I shall see you in the morning."

I grinned at him. I didn't want to let him go. I wanted to stay there with him. I wanted...him. An avalanche of carnal thoughts crossed my mind.

Hell's bells, Clemeny. Get it together.

"In the tomorrow...I mean, morning. Bye."

Lionheart huffed a laugh. "Bye."

Swallowing hard, I turned and left Temple Square.

From the first moment I'd met Sir Richard Spencer, I'd been attracted to him. In truth, I'd spent more than a moment lusting over him even before we were together. But it was one thing to lust over someone you thought you'd never have, and quite another to realize that you were actually on a path that could actually lead to…

My cheeks reddened at the thought.

But even so, my mind delighted at the idea. I was brave enough to slay a werewolf. Was I brave enough to bed one too?

CHAPTER 8
Nothing. No One. It's Nothing

I drove the steamauto across town to Harper's flat in Piccadilly. I had thought to leave a note with the doorman to inform Harper the auto was hers to take to Willowbrook, but as it turned out, Harper was home. Somehow, I imagined her perpetually in the office buried in paperwork when she wasn't with me.

When I reached her door, I heard Harper singing inside. Loudly. And giddily.

Grinning, I shook my head then knocked on the door.

"Coming," Harper called.

A moment later, she opened the door with a wide smile. "You're early. I thought you said eight—" Harper stopped cold when she saw me standing there.

I eyed her over. She was wearing a decidedly feminine dress, jewelry, and lip coloring. My eyes flicked to the room inside. She had laid out a fancy cape and reticule.

"Clemeny," she said, her voice filled with dismay. Behind her painted cheeks, I saw the color drain from her face. "What are you doing here?"

"Good evening, Elaine."

"Oh, I'm sorry," she said, a guilty expression crossing her face. "I was just…surprised."

"Why are you dressed like that?"

"I'm going…out."

"Out. Right. I guess I've come just in time. I'm headed out of town in the morning. I thought to leave you the steamauto in case you want to drive it to Willowbrook. It's parked outside."

"Oh, okay."

"So, you're going out?"

"Um. Yes. The theater."

I smiled. "What, Cabell finally convince you to give him a chance?"

Harper snort-laughed. "God no."

"Quartermain?"

"Oh. No. He's…no."

Harper and I stood staring at one another.

"I thought you'd be getting ready to go to Willowbrook," I said.

"I *am* ready," Harper said, a slight tone of indignation in her voice. Harper cleared her throat. "Thank you for bringing the steamauto. That was thoughtful of you. You aren't going to need it?"

"No. Lionheart is going to drive."

"Good. Good. I'm glad he's going. The druids...you just never know," Harper said as she fiddled with the door handle.

"You're right about that," I agreed.

"Yep," Harper said then cast a glance toward the stairwell behind me.

"Yep."

We stood there in silence for a long moment.

"All right, partner. See you when you get back," I said.

Harper nodded.

"I'll...I should go," I said, pointing behind me.

"Okay. Be safe."

"You too," I replied. I turned to leave, only pausing a moment to look back at Harper. She had a strange expression on her face. "You look pretty," I told her.

She let out a strangled half-yelp, half-something that sounded like a hiccup. "Thank you. You too. I mean, thank you. Not that you aren't pretty too—"

"Good night, Harper."

"Good night, Clemeny."

I gave her a little wave then headed back out into the night air. It was cool but not cold. It wasn't a far walk to

Vesta's Grotto from here. Pulling up my hood, I headed back across town.

All right, so Harper had a gentleman caller.

That was perfectly fine. That was her business. But she didn't need to act so weird about it.

I frowned then shook my head.

Harper could do whatever she liked. I had a case to worry about anyway. And a glowing dagger. Why in the hell did the dagger glow when I touched it? A sharp wind blew off the Thames. On it, I heard a soft voice.

Clemeny.

Clemeny Louvel.

"Yes, yes. I'm coming. I'm coming."

CHAPTER 9
First Impressions

The gate outside Vesta's Grotto squeaked when I swung it closed. I crossed the courtyard to the house. Sitting on a window seat inside the house, a furry black shape watched me, its eyes glimmering. The kitten leaped from the ledge, making the curtain sway. A moment later, the front door opened and Grand-mère appeared.

"Just in time, my girl. Just in time. Dinner is ready," she said then bent to pet the kitten, praising the feline's watchdog qualities in a slew of sweetly chirped French. She kissed the kitten on its head then set it back down.

Grand-mère turned and headed inside. The kitten scampered across the courtyard toward me.

"Tattletale," I said, pausing to pick her up. "And what have you been busy with today?" I asked, petting the little cat on her head. The kitten, whom I'd rescued from Lady Cabell, had grown from the tiny puffball I'd smuggled off the Fens to a long-legged creature Grand-mère had named Minuit.

The kitten purred sweetly, rubbing her head against my hand.

I slipped inside, closing the door behind me.

"Oranges and lemons, it's so cold outside," Grand-mère said. "You'd hardly think it's almost spring. You need to work in the office until this cold weather passes."

"I guess this means you won't approve of me leaving for Cornwall in the morning."

"Cornwall," Grand-mère protested. "What's in Cornwall?"

"The Cornish," I replied, hanging my cape on the hook just inside the door.

My nose led me to the kitchen where rosemary chicken, fresh-baked sourdough bread, and roasted potatoes sat on the table. Grand-mère worked busily setting out the plates.

"Cornwall. Is Harper going?"

"No. She's headed north. I left the auto with her."

"Then how are you going to get there?"

"Professor Spencer."

"Oh," Grand-mère said, the delight evident in her voice. "And how is the good professor?"

I chuckled. "Very well, Grand-mère."

"I was so disappointed to see Edwin go, but Professor Spencer is *such* a gentleman. A truly refined man, a scholar. He's such a marvelous catch, Clemeny. You've done very well."

I had not yet had the heart in me to inform Grand-mère that my refined gentleman was, in fact, a were-wolf. She'd been so pleased with him that I didn't want to shatter her illusions. The truth was, I hardly knew myself how the relationship between Richard and I was going to work. It was too complicated to trouble Grand-mère with. So, for now, it was better to say nothing.

Grand-mère loaded me up a plate.

I gave Minuit one last pat and a kiss on her furry little head then set her down and went to wash my hands.

"Clemeny, pour us some wine, my dear," Grand-mère called.

I pulled down two glasses, poured us both a white wine, then joined Grand-mère at the table. As I relaxed into my seat, I felt the weight of the day on me. I was tired. And hungry.

"*Santé*," Grand-mère said, lifting her glass in a toast.

"*Santé*. It looks delicious."

"All for you, my girl. All for you."

I sipped the wine and looked out the window. The moonlight was shimmering on the leaves of the trees outside. It was a pretty sight. But tomorrow, I would go to Cornwall. And what would I find there?

"So, why are you going to Cornwall?" Grand-mère asked.

"Someone tried to assassinate the Queen today."

Grand-mère swore in French. "Someone Cornish?"

"Not exactly. But it's a place to start."

"Queen Victoria, always gallivanting about like she's a commoner. But, my dear, what does it have to do with you?"

"I suppose they hope I'll find her would-be assassin before he strikes again."

Grand-mère clicked her tongue. "I'm glad Professor Spencer is going with you."

"I can handle myself, Grand-mère."

She laughed. "Don't I know it, my dear. Don't I know it. But it's always good to have a partner. In work…and in life," she said then winked at me.

"Grand-mère," I said, rolling my eyes.

"Even Quinn knew that. How is little Isadora? You were in Twickenham this morning."

"She's very pretty. Loud but pretty."

Grand-mère laughed. "One day you too will have a loud but pretty babe. Oh, Clemeny, I can't wait for that day," Grand-mère said, setting down her wine glass long enough to clap her hands and send up a prayer.

"Oh!" she said, breaking off her imploration. "How is Professor Spencer's young ward? Jericho, isn't it?"

"Also loud but adorable."

"Mischievous little cherub," Grand-mère said.

Lycan. Mischievous lycan.

"And how do the two of you get on?" Grand-mère asked as she poured me some more wine.

"Me and Jericho?"

Grand-mère nodded.

"Very well. I'm quite fond of the boy."

"Oh, that's very good, very good indeed. Poor motherless child. And Professor Spencer, such a good man to take him in. Such a learned, refined, and godly man. Why yes, it's an excellent thing you're traveling together. You never know what could come of it."

"You're right. Suppose he'll propose to me tomorrow?" I asked teasingly.

Grand-mère laughed. "Perhaps he will, and then what will you do, my girl?" she retorted playfully.

No. There was no chance that was going to happen.

"Grand-mère, you must give things time."

"Time?" Grand-mère said, then blew air through her lips. "I was madly in love with Grand-père the moment I saw him. Of course, that doesn't happen to everyone. But it happened to me."

My mind drifted back to the first moment Quinn had introduced me to Sir Richard Spencer. Lionheart had been in his office at King's College. We'd gone to see him based on the slim hope that he'd give us some tip on a case.

"Just hang back," Quinn had told me. "Lionheart is adamant about staying out of pack trouble. But one can hope. We just need a lead."

Quinn knocked hard on the office door.

Then, we waited.

And waited.

"Maybe he's at Temple Square," I whispered.

Quinn shook his head. "No. He's here. And he can hear me. Sir Richard, a word?" Quinn called to the closed door.

We waited a moment longer, and then I heard a shuffle inside the office. A moment later, the door had opened to reveal the most handsome creature I had ever seen. Dressed in a fine tweed suit, his spectacles perched on his nose, that loose lock of blond hair hanging over one eye, he was fine-looking enough to catch any lady's attention. It didn't hurt that he'd also undone his tie and unbuttoned the top of his shirt.

I swallowed hard and tried to focus.

"I'm quite busy, Agent Briarwood," Lionheart told Quinn.

"I just need a moment."

Lionheart had sighed, but then he looked around Quinn at me. "And this is?"

"Agent Louvel," Quinn answered.

"Does Agent Louvel have a first name?" Lionheart asked, looking at me with those deep, wolfy eyes. I'd felt like I wanted to melt into my boots.

"It hardly—" Quinn began.

"Clemeny."

Lionheart studied me carefully then stepped back, motioning for us to come in.

Quinn directed me to take a seat opposite Lionheart's desk; Quinn sat in the chair beside me. Richard returned to his seat.

"I'm hoping you can help us," Quinn told Lionheart who was still looking at me.

"Where are you from, Clemeny Louvel?" Lionheart asked me.

"Saint Clement Danes. Where are you from, Professor Spencer?"

"The twelfth-century."

We grinned at one another.

Lionheart tapped his fingers on his desk, and after a long moment, he rose and went to his cabinet. Removing a bottle, he poured us all a drink. He set the cups down in front of us then lifted his glass.

"God save the Queen," he toasted.

"God save the Queen," Quinn and I replied, lifting our cups.

Quinn set his cup down without drinking. I took a sip and then another.

"Louvel. French. I believe the name means 'little wolf.' Did you know that, Agent Louvel?" Lionheart asked.

"I did. It's the reason I took the job. I was going to hunt vampires, but it wouldn't have matched."

Lionheart smirked. "You must be the one they're calling Little Red."

"Is that what they call me?"

"It is."

"*Little* Red. Well, looks can be deceiving," I said, sipping the drink.

"Indeed they can," Lionheart replied.

"Speaking of which, despite all apparent signs of your disinterest in our case, we need your help," I told the werewolf.

"Do you?"

"Perhaps. Depends on what you know."

Lionheart gestured for me to continue.

"Cyril is working with an airship pirate, making quick cash on human trafficking. We need to put a stop to such an abomination. He has a contact in the Dark District, but we don't know who. Can you help?"

Lionheart removed his spectacles and looked closely at me. After a long moment, he said, "The Broken Violin." Pulling out a scrap of paper, he jotted down an address which he handed to me. "Pub on the east bank. Start there."

I moved to take the paper.

Lionheart held onto the note for a long moment.

I met his eyes.

"Thank you, Sir Richard," I said.

"You're welcome, Agent Louvel."

Quinn rose. "Thank you, Lionheart."

Lionheart, whose eyes were still on me, gave Quinn a slight nod then let go of the paper.

"I'll see you again," I said with a sly grin.

At that, Lionheart smirked then sat back in his seat.

Stuffing the paper into my vest, I rose. Quinn and I headed to the door. As I exited, I looked back at that old werewolf who was studying me over his glass of Scotch. Meeting my gaze, he raised his cup in a toast.

I winked at him then closed the door behind me.

"Well, that was awkward," Quinn said.

"For who?"

Quinn laughed. "For me. But we got what we were after. Well done, partner. Well done," he said then clapped me on the back. "Lionheart never talks to me. Now I know why."

"And that is?"

"I'm not pretty enough. That hurts my feelings."

We both laughed then headed on our way.

"More wine?" Grand-mère asked, shaking me from my thoughts.

I nodded.

All this time, Lionheart had been right in front of me, the connection between us instant. And I had totally missed it. Until now.

The dinner passed quickly, and feeling drunk on food—and maybe a little too much wine—I headed upstairs. I packed a travel bag then slipped on a nightdress. I slid into bed. A moment later, Minuit hopped onto the bed. Purring, she snuggled close beside me. I gave her a pat then turned and looked at my bedside table. Lying there, I spotted the star metal dagger. Reaching out, I touched the metal. A soft blue glow filled the room. But in the dim of night, I noticed something new. The metal didn't just glow blue. There were shapes in the light, twirling designs and sparkles.

"Okay, that's weird," I whispered into the darkness.

Minuit let out a tired meow as if she were answering me in her sleep.

I chuckled then closed my eyes.

Soon, I would get answers.

Soon.

CHAPTER 10
Of Pain au Chocolat, Peanuts, and Bones

I slid into the auto, smiling at Jericho who was sitting in the back seat.

"My grand-mère sent these," I said, passing back a basket of *pain au chocolat* to the boy whose mood instantly brightened. He took the basket greedily, dipping into it at once.

"Jericho," Lionheart called lightly in reminder.

"Oh! Right. Thank you, Clemeny," the boy said. From the sound of his muffled voice, he was already a bite too late.

"You're welcome," I said with a chuckle then smiled at Lionheart who was grinning in spite of himself.

"I hope you saved one for us," Lionheart said then pulled the auto onto the London street.

I patted my satchel.

"For you, *pain au chocolat*. For me, these," I said, pulling out my pack of ginger.

"You know, if the packs ever learn you actually have a weakness…" he said teasingly.

"Weakness? Did you know I flew in an airship—*with Lily Stargazer*—and managed to hold down my breakfast? A little nausea won't stop me."

At that, Lionheart laughed. "No doubt."

I grinned.

"You flew with Lily Stargazer?"

I nodded.

Lionheart harrumphed, impressed.

"I know, right?"

He reached across the seat and took my hand, giving it a soft squeeze.

"So, today we are looking to find druids who don't want to be found. Where to begin?" Lionheart asked.

"Salisbury."

"Stonehenge?"

I nodded. "It's a start."

"You aren't going to find any druids there," Jericho said absently between munches.

I looked back. "What do you mean?"

He shrugged. "If you're looking for someone who doesn't want to be found, why would they be where you expect to find them?"

I chuckled. "You have a point. Have a better suggestion?"

Jericho shrugged. "No."

I looked at Lionheart. "How about you, professor?"

He shook his head. "I'll leave this to you."

"Then to Salisbury."

It sounded like a joke. A lycan, a werewolf, and a werewolf hunter set out on a road trip to track down druids and smoke out evil faeries. What could possibly go wrong?

IT TOOK THE ENTIRE DAY TO REACH THE WINDY FLATS OF Salisbury where Stonehenge was located. Given we had to stop twice to get Jericho something to eat, and three more times for the child to make a toilette out of the high weeds growing at the side of the road, I was almost relieved when the ancient stone monolith came into sight.

Almost.

Somehow, I had conjured an image in my mind that Stonehenge was a place of worship for the druids, a solemn, empty spot where the mist wove around the stones, and the druids chanted their ancient Celtic wizardry.

What I hadn't expected were the picnickers.

And croquet matches.

And drink and food carts to replenish the same.

No druids.

A small parking area was situated not far from the ancient monoliths. Lionheart pulled up alongside another steamauto, three carriages, a steamcycle, and a very large wagon painted with the colors of Trinity College on the side.

When we got out of the auto, I stared across the green.

There, the ancient stone circle sat in all her glory. The ring of ancient stones buzzed with energy. The ground below my feet pulsed with life. Every hair on my head tingled.

And all around the stones, gaily dressed revelers, ladies with parasols, and gentlemen in beautiful suits, picnicked and frolicked. Someone had spread out a full afternoon tea service on one of the fallen capstones. Ladies giggled and fanned themselves under the warm spring sun as they leaned against the ancient stones. Not far away, a group of children were playing croquet. A boy and his father toyed with a kite. On the other side of the stones, I spotted what looked like an excavation. There, gentlemen in Trinity College colors were digging into one of the burial mounds not far from the stones.

No druids.

No answers.

"Nothing," I whispered.

"Look," Jericho said, pointing as he tugged on my sleeve.

Hoping for some good news, I followed his lead. He was pointing to a vendor cart from which I caught the scent of roasting peanuts.

"Clemeny, Sir Richard, I'm starving. May I have a parcel?" he asked as sweetly as possible.

Swallowing my disappointment, I smiled at the boy. He really was a sweet thing. His golden hair shimmered in the warm sunlight, his dark eyes wide and innocent.

"Of course," I told Jericho then took the child's hand. We headed to the vendor.

As we made our way, I debated what to do. It was a bad idea to bring Lionheart here. I hated it when a case didn't go well. I didn't want him to see me struggle, not with this. I needed Richard to see me as his equal. Failing to find any clues was just...embarrassing.

"How many, miss?" the vendor asked.

I looked over my shoulder at Lionheart who was studying the excavation.

"One, please," I said then smiled down at Jericho. "A large one. And a lemonade."

Despite the fact that my mouth wanted to eat, my stomach had ridden far too long in the auto to justify the risk. It was bad enough that I had botched my case. Throwing up would add to the embarrassment.

The man handed the parcel and drink to Jericho while I dug in my pocket for some coin.

"Thank you, Clemeny," Jericho whispered.

I ruffled his hair, then the two of us joined Lionheart.

"Let's speak to them," Lionheart said, motioning to the men working at the dig. "Will you pardon me in asking to take—as you say in the agency—the lead on this one?"

I chuckled. "Considering your service to the crown far outranks mine in tenure, be my guest."

"Ah, the age jokes never grow old."

"Are you certain?"

Lionheart winked at me.

Lionheart took my arm, and we crossed to the site of the dig. The men were busy excavating one of the burial mounds that dotted the landscape around the circle of stones. The sight unnerved me. This was a tomb, not a historical curiosity. And lay people didn't know what lingered on the other side of that doorway they were shoveling into.

"Good afternoon, gentlemen," Lionheart said. Alpha of the Templars no more, Professor Richard Spencer was on the case.

One of the workers jostled a man wearing tan

trousers and matching hat; the man was dressed as if he were on a dig in Egypt.

"Sir, there is a gentleman here," the worker told the man.

The stranger turned around. He eyed Lionheart over. "Good afternoon, sir. May I help you?"

"Sir Richard Spencer. King's College."

"Oh, very good, very good," he said, extending his hand to Lionheart. "Professor Eckhart. Trinity College. A pleasure to meet you."

Lionheart gave me a sidelong glance then said, "My *wife* and I were passing through and noticed your dig. I say, quite an impressive project you have underway."

"Indeed, indeed," the man agreed. He looped his thumbs in his belt loops then tipped forward, extending his stomach proudly. "We've unearthed two torcs already this morning. I believe we are getting close to the body."

"Whose body?" I asked.

"Someone of great importance. A chieftain. Maybe even a druid."

"Ah, there are the druids you were looking for," Lionheart said, giving me a playful wink.

I rolled my eyes at him.

"We were hoping we might catch sight of the druids, in fact. No luck it seems," Lionheart said.

"Well," Professor Eckhart mused, "they do come

around at midsummer, I'm told. But you won't be seeing one today unless you'd like to dig."

"I'll dig," Jericho offered.

"Ah, that's a good lad," the professor said good-naturedly. "Lucas, grab that boy a shovel and set him to work. We can't find the owner of all this treasure," the man said, motioning to the table where some artifacts lay. "Maybe your son will bring us some luck. Would you really like to try, young man?"

Jericho nodded vehemently.

Professor Eckhart looked at Lionheart who nodded in approval.

The worker, Lucas, handed Jericho a small shovel and led him to the mound.

"Come, see what I've found," Professor Eckhart said, motioning us to a table where the dig finds had been laid out. "What's your specialty, Professor Spencer? I'm a Celtic scholar. Not fashionable, I know. I should join my colleagues in Greece, but I'm something of a nationalist."

Lionheart chuckled. "Then you are among friends."

"My *husband* is an expert on the Templars," I interjected, giving Lionheart a playful look.

He smirked in reply.

"Oh, good. Good," Professor Eckhart exclaimed.

"Any chance you've uncovered a goblet?" Lionheart asked.

The professor laughed. "Still hunting the grail, eh? Unfortunately, no," the man said then lifted a silver wrist torc. The piece was beautifully crafted. "Fine Celtic smithwork, though. And some Roman coins. Dagger, though it's much corroded," he said as he lifted each piece, showing it to Lionheart and me.

The discoveries were fascinating, but I had a distinct feeling that they should have been left where they were found.

Lionheart lifted the coin. "Do you think it was contemporary to the other pieces?"

"No. The rest of the artifacts suggest the body was laid in the ground after the retreat of the Romans…" the Professor continued, but I got distracted as my skin rose in goosebumps.

A soft breeze blew across the windy plane, ruffling my hair.

Clemeny.

Clemeny Louvel.

I turned and looked all around.

First to the stones.

Then to the mounds.

Clemeny.

Clemeny, come.

Come home.

I turned and scanned the landscape, narrowing my gaze, looking past all the revelers and eyeing the land with my mooneye. There was magic everywhere. And everyone was missing it. The stones shimmered with opalescent light, and there was a strange aura around them. The monoliths wavered. They had one foot in this world, one foot in the Otherworld.

But I saw more.

As I looked, I saw shimmering silver light trailing away from the henge. Lines of energy moved through the ground. They traveled to the mounds and then beyond, spreading like a web across the land.

I had seen this once before. Lily Stargazer had used it to make her airship speed over the land.

A group of children cheered as one of the players whacked their ball through a wicket. Ladies gossiped and laughed as they drank tea. Everyone was so oblivious to the magic around them.

I stared at—and into—the stones. For a brief moment, the image in front of me shifted. For just a brief moment, a woman appeared at the center of the stones. She wore long blue robes. I could not see her face clearly, but I knew her gaze was on me. She beckoned to me.

I stared at her, then past her. There, on the rise in the distance, I saw great Glastonbury Tor, which was dozens of miles from here. I saw a silver line of energy running from the ancient henge to a place of legend:

Glastonbury. Just like I'd dreamed when I'd stayed at Cabell Manor.

"...I'd place it well after Boudicca's rebellion, but—" Professor Eckhart was saying when his worker, Lucas, called out to him.

"Professor Eckhart. Sir, come look," Lucas shouted.

Worried about Jericho, I turned from the vision.

"What is it?" Professor Eckhart called.

"The boy," Lucas answered.

Oh, damn.

I turned to Lionheart, both of us wearing panicked expressions. We rushed to the dig.

There, Jericho stood with his hands on his hips, his small shovel in one hand, a smile on his face. In the dirt in front of him, one could make out what looked like a bone.

"You found it!" Professor Eckhart exclaimed, giving Jericho a clap on the back.

Jericho smiled up at Lionheart then to me.

I returned his happy gaze.

"Well done," Lionheart told the boy who beamed at him.

They exchanged a warm glance.

My heart did a little dance.

"Your son has a nose for archeology," Professor Eckhart said, smiling back at me. "Just like his father."

I opened my mouth then closed it again. What could I say?

"Well done, Jericho," I told him, giving him a hug.

"You'll need to dine with us tonight. We have a club in Salisbury. Join us," Professor Eckhart said.

"I'm afraid we can't," I said. "We're on our way to Glastonbury."

"Shame. Shame," Professor Eckhart said. He removed his fancy explorer's hat and set it on Jericho's head. "Well, maybe one day you'll join my crew again, young man. In the meantime, keep that as a memento of your success on the expedition."

Jericho touched the rim of the cap. "Thank you, sir."

"We should be off? To Glastonbury?" Lionheart asked me, a quizzical expression on his face.

I nodded.

Lionheart nodded then turned back to the professor. "It was a pleasure to meet you, sir." He gave the man a short bow.

"The pleasure was mine, Sir Richard. Your son saved me a week's work," he added with a laugh. "Madame," he said then nodded to me.

I inclined my head to him, then the three of us headed away from the stones, back toward the auto.

"Well done," I told Jericho. "However did you know where to dig?"

"It was easy," Jericho told me.

"Easy? How?"

"I could smell the bones in the earth," he explained simply. "I just...dug them up."

At that, I looked at Lionheart. After a moment, we both laughed.

"Well, I think you've earned another lemonade," Lionheart told the boy.

"And more peanuts?"

"Yes," I said.

"Yay," Jericho called merrily then ran off ahead of us.

Lionheart extended his arm to me. "Well, *wife*, we're headed to Glastonbury?"

I chuckled. "So we are, *husband*."

"And why is that?"

I nodded. "Let's just say I have a hunch."

"Then I guess we'd better follow it."

"Clemeny?" Jericho called. He was standing at the vendor's cart once more. "Clemeny, the man needs money," he yelled then looked at Lionheart. "Please."

I giggled then turned to Lionheart. "You really are doing a wonderful job with him. He was a broken child when I found him."

Lionheart sighed. "It isn't easy, but I'm trying. I care for the boy. Much more than I ever thought I could."

"Well, you are lion-hearted, after all," I said with a grin.

"Clemeny!" Jericho called again. The child's hunger outweighed his patience. It was a trouble I understood well.

Lionheart squeezed my hand. He turned toward Jericho. "Patience and manners, Jericho. My *wife* and I are coming," he said, winking at me.

At that moment, I thought my heart might burst with joy.

CHAPTER 11
Abbey House

We left the ancient monolith in Salisbury and headed to Glastonbury. Jericho fell asleep in the back along the way.

"What do you expect to find?" Lionheart asked me.

"I'm not sure. Once, long ago, you asked me if I had ever gone to the summer country. Do you remember?"

Lionheart nodded.

"Why did you ask me that?"

"Creeping around as long as I have—as you never forget to remind me—one encounters other preternaturals. Long ago, when I was searching for the grail, I met a woman who had the same light and a similar flowery scent that you have. I encountered her, albeit briefly, at the ruins of a castle in the Westlands."

"Who was she? What was she? Was she human?"

Lionheart shook his head. "I don't know. She was there and gone. But the magic that surrounded her filled the air with the strange perfume that encapsulates you."

"Strange?"

"Unusual."

"Unusual?"

"Divine."

"Ah, that's better."

Lionheart grinned, but then his expression turned serious. "You must be cautious. I believe you have some hopes pinned on what you may find. Am I right?"

He was. Buried below my interest in solving my case, my desire to protect Victoria and the realm, was my hope that seeking out the druids would finally provide me with some answers about myself.

"Yes."

"There is a reason the Red Capes do not intermingle with the druids. Your desire for answers could put you at risk."

"I'm not worried. After all, I have a werewolf at my side. What's the worst that could happen?"

"They could shoot me with a silver bullet and haul you off to the Otherworld."

"Are you always so grim?"

"That's why I'm still alive."

"Well, I'll keep your warning in mind."

"You know, it seems rather counterintuitive to go to the ruins of an Abbey in search of druids."

"We're not going to Glastonbury Abbey."

"Then where are we going, Agent Louvel?"

"I think…I think we're going to Avalon."

It was already dusk when the ruins atop Glastonbury Tor came into sight. The sunset soaked the sky with hues of magenta, orange, and deep purple. The moment I saw the place, my whole body started to buzz. There was a strange ringing in my ears that I couldn't shake.

Lionhead gazed at me.

"Are you all right?"

No.

"Yes."

"Liar."

"I just… Do you feel anything?"

Lionheart looked thoughtful. "Yes," he said simply.

He turned the auto down a narrow drive that wound around the Tor.

"Where are you going?"

"Abbey House," Lionheart said.

"Abbey House?"

He nodded. "You are in luck, Agent Louvel. Your new beau is of wide acquaintance."

I grinned. *My new beau.*

As we drove down the road, a nervous feeling rocked my stomach. I felt the urgent need to do…something. But what? Anxiety made me shift in my seat. Soon, a manor appeared on the horizon. Lionheart pulled the auto up to the front.

"I'll be but a moment," he said, then slipped out and went to the door.

I watched as the butler appeared in the doorframe, silhouetted by golden light from within the manor.

"Where are we?" Jericho asked groggily. He'd been sleeping for most of the ride, the explorer's cap still on his head.

"Glastonbury," I told him.

He yawned tiredly.

I reached back, pulled off the hat, then smoothed down his wispy blond hair, which was jutting out in all directions. I set the cap on his head once more.

"Lord, I'm hungry," he said as he rubbed his eyes. "Will Sir Richard get us something to eat? Who is that man he's talking to?"

A second man had appeared at the door. This gentleman was just a slip of a thing, wearing spectacles that were too big for his face. The man clapped Lionheart on the back, and the two headed our way, the butler following behind.

"I don't know."

"Which part? The food or the man?"

"Neither."

Jericho chuckled. "You're funny."

The butler hurried ahead and opened the door. I tipped my chin to Jericho, motioning for him to follow me out of the auto.

"Thank you," I told the butler then took Jericho's hand.

"Sir, may I present Agent Clemeny Louvel. And this is my ward, Jericho. Clemeny, this is John Fry Reeves, a fellow antiquarian."

"Mister Reeves," I said, giving the man a polite curtsey.

"I scolded Sir Richard for not letting me know he was coming," the elderly man told me. "I have some papers for you, Sir Richard. I was planning to pack them up and send them on to you at King's College."

"I apologize. It was an impromptu trip. Agent Louvel is working on a case that led her here."

"*Agent* Louvel, you say," the old man said, eyeing me over. He nodded thoughtfully. "Rude Mechanicals business, I suppose. How did you get yourself mixed up with them?"

"Agent Louvel is very persuasive."

He chuckled softly. "I bet," he said, raising then lowering his eyebrows. "And this is your ward. Jericho, you said?" he said, bending to examine the boy who gripped my hand a little more tightly and took half a step behind me.

"Yes," Lionheart replied. "Jericho, please say hello to Mister Reeves."

"Hello, Mister Reeves," Jericho said shyly.

I pitied Jericho. He had lived a life sheltered away from the world. Ever since he'd come to London from the Fens, his life had been nothing but change. Lionheart had the double task of raising a lycan, but also helping a child acclimate to the world outside the swamps. It was no easy task. I'd done my best to help where I could. I never missed a day, stopping in to see the boy. Afwyn had handed the child to me, making me promise to watch over him. My heart went out to the boy. I knew what it felt like to be an orphan. But more than that, I cared for the child.

Mister Reeves chuckled, his manner friendly. "Sweet little chap. And have you been off expedition?" he asked Jericho, motioning to the hat.

"I dug up a bone today," Jericho said softly, still half-hiding behind me.

"You did? Well, very good. Very good. Why don't you all come in? I'll have Franklin see to some rooms for you. And I bet a bite to eat wouldn't hurt anyone," the old man said, smiling at Jericho.

"I hate to impose. I am sure there is an inn nearby," I said.

"Not at all, Agent Louvel. Sir Richard is an old friend. I've been hunting Joseph of Arimathea, you see. With Sir Richard being a grail scholar, our paths have crossed many times. Yet here we are, both of us still looking, both of us still empty-handed."

Lionheart laughed. "True."

"Well, time will tell if either of us can solve our riddles," the man added as he motioned for us to follow him inside.

The house was nicely appointed. A stately, gentleman's estate, it had a beautiful foyer with hardwood floors and polished wood panel walls. A chandelier hung over a center drum table upon which sat a bouquet of fresh flowers. Their scent perfumed the place.

"Let's go to the sitting room. Franklin, please have a supper prepared for our guests. And ensure Elizabeth prepares some rooms for the night," Mister Reeves told his butler who nodded.

Mister Reeves led us to a sitting room which boasted an ornate fireplace, tapestries, richly upholstered furniture, and a view of Glastonbury ruins framed by a massive window. The view almost looked like a painting.

"Clemeny," Lionheart called, motioning for me to join him at the window.

Leading Jericho, who was still holding my hand, I went to him.

The window was at least ten feet in height. The view framed the arching ruins of Glastonbury, which were soaked in the rosy hues of the sunset. As I stared out at the place, my mooneye started messing with me. The stones of the ruins shifted and wavered, there one moment and gone the next. I narrowed my gaze. Beyond the sight of my good eye, but evident with my mooneye, I saw the spirits that haunted the place. Balls of fairy light, glimmering in shades of blue, green, silver, and gold, floated throughout the ruins. The magic emanating from the place was more than I could stand. Stonehenge was nothing compared to this.

"A heap of stones now but once an important center. I tracked Joseph of Arimathea here, Agent Louvel, then lost him," Mister Reeves said.

"And with him, the grail," Lionheart added.

"I don't like it," Jericho said, surprising me.

I looked down at him.

He was scrunching up his face at the sight. The expression was far too reminiscent of his birth mother, Lady Charlotte, for my liking.

"And why not?" Lionheart asked.

"Too many fairies."

I raised an eyebrow at the boy then looked at Lionheart who turned his gaze to me. But why should we be surprised? Jericho had been raised by elementals. Of course, he'd been taught to see the Otherworld.

Mister Reeves laughed. "The place does have a haunt to it, doesn't it, lad? Not to worry, though. This old house is warded."

"Warded?" I asked.

Mister Reeves chuckled. "I bought this place from one of your employers, Agent. A member of the Rude Mechanicals built it. Superstitious lot. But I'm sure you know that already."

"To be frank, I'm rather surprised you know about my employers, sir."

"When you're in the trade of hunting down the strange and unusual, it won't be long before you bump into the strange and unusual," he said then clapped Lionheart on the shoulder. "Brandy, Sir Richard?"

"Yes, please."

"And you, Agent Louvel?"

"Please."

"And let me see what I have for the young man," he said then crossed the room to the drink cart. "How about cherries and limes, Master Jericho?"

Jericho looked up at me.

I shrugged. "Try it."

"Yes, sir."

Master Reeves smiled, nodded, then went to work. A moment later, he returned with drinks for all of us. He handed Jericho a bubbling drink filled with candied cherries and limes then turned to Lionheart. "A toast, old friend?"

"To Joseph of Arimathea," Lionheart said, lifting his cup.

"To Joseph of Arimathea, wherever he may rest," Mister Reeves replied, and we clicked our glasses together.

I took a sip, hoping the brandy would calm my nerves. This place had all of my senses on edge. Leave it to the Rude Mechanicals to build a house on the fringe of the Otherworld.

"Sir Richard, since I have you here, would you mind having a look at a manuscript I've recovered? It was found hidden in a crate in a hayloft, of all things. What luck! I've been trying to work out the letters, but they're so faded. I can't make out whether it says fated or faith," Master Reeves said, motioning for Lionheart to examine a yellowing tome lying on a nearby desk.

Lionheart met my eye for a moment, nodded to me, then joined Mister Reeves.

I sat down on an ottoman near the massive window. Jericho, who was holding his drink with both hands, stared outside.

"Come here," I said softly, pulling him to sit on my knee. "What do you see out there?" I whispered.

"Fairies. They're everywhere."

"Fairies or spirits?"

"I can see the fairies. Are there spirits too?"

"Yes."

"I can't see them. You can?"

I nodded.

"This place reminds of me of the fen."

"Why?"

"Because it's…loose."

"Loose. Yes, that's a good word to describe it."

We both looked out at the scene.

"Do you miss the fens?"

Jericho nodded. "I miss Anwyn…and the others. But I like being in London with Lionheart. And you."

"I'm glad. One day, once things are a little more settled, we can return to the fens and see them."

"No."

"Why not?"

"Because they are gone now."

"Gone?"

Jericho nodded. "Into there…somewhere," he said, motioning with his chin.

"How do you know?"

"I just know."

I stared at the ruins. I was sure Jericho was right. Anwyn said they were barely holding on. Maybe the boy was all that was binding them to this world. Now that he was gone, had the elementals—no, gods—receded into the Otherworld too?

"Clemeny," the boy whispered in a low voice.

"Yes?"

"I don't like limes."

I looked over my shoulder. Mister Reeves and Lionheart were poring over the manuscript. Taking Jericho's drink from his hand, I polished it off then handed it back to him. He was right. The tart limes had overpowered the cherries. Bless Mister Reeves, at least he had tried.

I sipped my brandy once more, washing out the tart taste.

"Thank you," Jericho said with a whisper.

"You were right. That was awful," I said with a grin.

Jericho giggled.

I wrapped my arm around his waist and hugged him close to me. I felt the press of his small body against mine. It filled me with warmth and peace, my nerves suddenly calming. "Of course."

"Master Reeves, dinner for your guests, sir," Franklin called from the door.

"Very good," Master Reeves called. "Shall we?"

I rose, and with Jericho's hand in mine, we turned and headed to the dining room.

CHAPTER 12
Past and Future

Dinner passed pleasantly. Jericho was lost to his meal. I had to smother my laugh as Franklin, the butler, stared as Jericho ate with exceptional vigor. The butler wasn't adequately prepared to feed a ravenous lycan. He repeatedly stepped forward to take Jericho's plate, but the boy simply asked for a little more. Again. And again. And again.

Mister Reeves was busy picking Lionheart's mind about this or that obscure piece of research, while I watched and listened to the interactions between the two.

For the moment, I felt surprisingly relaxed. Happy, even. My eyes went from Lionheart to Jericho. Yes, I felt truly happy.

After he finished his fifth serving, Jericho finally sat back in his seat and yawned.

"Tired?" I whispered to him.

He nodded.

"Mister Reeves, I'll take Jericho and get him settled in for the night."

"Of course, Agent. Franklin, would you show Agent Louvel and Sir Richard's ward to their rooms."

"Of course, sir," the butler replied, moving forward to pull out my chair.

Lionheart rose. "Will you pardon me for a moment, John. I'll see to my fam—to them, then return."

"Naturally, naturally," Mister Reeves said then rose. "And I'll go see if the cook has anything sweet to eat."

"Something sweet?" Jericho said, perking up a little.

I didn't blame him, but I also didn't blame Lionheart when he said, "It's time to settle in for the night, my boy."

Jericho huffed a little, but only a little.

Franklin led us to the second floor of the elegant house.

"You will be here, Sir Richard," the butler said, motioning to a door. "And your ward is in the room adjacent to you. There is an interior door. Agent Louvel will be across the hall. Shall I send up the maid for you, Agent?"

God, no.

"No. Thank you."

"Very good. Sir Richard, we don't have a valet, but if you need—"

"We're well. Thank you," Lionheart said.

"As you wish," the butler replied with a polite bow.

"I'll let you get changed then come back to tuck you in," I told Jericho.

"All right," he said. "But don't forget."

"I won't."

I smiled at Lionheart who was looking tenderly at the boy. "Come along," Lionheart said, reaching out for Jericho's hand.

Lionheart and I exchanged a glance then I headed to my own room.

The room they'd given me was small but charming. The bed was covered in a feminine, flower-embroidered coverlet. There was a vase of daffodils on the bedside table. I hadn't expected to find myself in some fancy manor house again. I figured I'd be in some bloody fisticuffs with a faerie by now. But the turnabout in circumstance was welcome. The fireplace had been lit; it popped and crackled.

I went to the window and looked out. The sun had sunk below the horizon, and the ruins in the distance were illuminated by the glow of the moon and the strange ethereal light that clung to the stones. Still, the image wavered. The fog had rolled in, but the sky was full of stars.

As I stared out the window, my senses were set on edge. The soles of my feet itched.

Clemeny.

Clemeny Louvel.

I inhaled deeply, slowly. I pulled the faerie's blade from my belt. It glowed blue. The bright light cast a reflection on the windowpane.

I was here.

Now what?

I turned from the window and went to my bed. Setting aside the dagger, I slipped off my belt, removing my pistols, knife, gadgets, and Fenton. I tossed my red cape on the back of a chair, pulling off my leather vest as well. Wearing a white button shirt and leather trousers, I sat down at the end of the bed and debated on what to do. I could change into the dress Grand-mère had insisted I pack and go to the parlor and sip brandy for the rest of the night.

I could do that.

And then afterward, I could come upstairs.

With Richard.

And...

My stomach twisted into a knot.

When I'd asked Lionheart to join me on the trip into the west country, I hadn't expected Jericho would come.

I wasn't sorry he was there. I loved the child, and I didn't want him to feel scared and alone. It was just... since that autumn, things between Lionheart and me had been growing toward something. Something entirely new for me. Whatever I'd felt toward Edwin, I felt it a thousandfold for Lionheart. I had made the right decision. And now, I was ready for more.

But there was the case to be considered.

The Queen's life was at stake.

And...I looked out the window once more.

And there was that.

For the first time in my entire life, it felt like the answer to my oldest question was within my grasp.

It would be easier to slip into that pretty dress lying at the bottom of my bag and pretend answers weren't right outside the door. Literally.

I knew what I needed to do.

I smoothed my hair back, quickly pulled it into a long braid. Leaving my room, I crossed the hall and knocked on the door. "It's Clemeny," I called.

"Come in," Lionheart replied.

I opened the door and went inside. Crossing Lionheart's room, I went to the adjacent chamber where I found Jericho in bed, Lionheart sitting at his bedside.

The boy smiled at me.

Lionheart looked over his shoulder, that lock of blond hair hanging just above his eye.

I stared at them.

My life had been so strange. Grand-mère had done everything to give me a home, to love me, to make me feel like there was nothing odd about anything. But there was. There always had been. Just below my skin, I'd always been different.

I looked at the pair before me, both of them smiling at me, both of them with a tell-tale flicker of red in their eyes. And for the very first time, I felt like I belonged. I belonged here with them.

Whatever was outside the doors of Abbey House didn't matter.

In this room, I saw my future.

"Time to sleep," I said sweetly, my voice cracking as I hid the emotion that wanted to bubble to the surface. I crossed the room and sat down beside him.

"You'll be just across the hall?" Jericho asked me.

I nodded.

"I'll join Master Reeves for a bit then come back upstairs," Lionheart told him.

"All right," Jericho said then slipped further into his bed. He yawned tiredly. "Clemeny?"

"Yes?"

"The fairies keep looking at you. Be careful. You can't always trust them."

"I have nothing to fear. I have a werewolf and a lycan to keep me safe."

Jericho laughed softly.

I smoothed his hair then kissed him on the forehead.

The boy sighed contentedly then after a few moments, his breathing became slow and deep.

"Fairies?" Lionheart whispered.

"The ruins. There are fairy globes. A lot of them."

"So, is your hunch right?"

"We shall see."

"Are you… What are you going to do?"

I sighed. "Well, I suppose I need to go see to the matter."

"I'll get my things."

"No," I said then paused. "I think…I think I need to go alone."

"Clemeny—"

"I'll be all right."

"You don't even know what's out there."

"Fairies. Didn't you hear?"

"I did. But besides that."

"Maybe I'm a fairy. I've never tried to shrink down. After all, I am *Little* Red. Maybe I can get smaller," I said then closed my eyes and scrunched up my brow.

"You look like you're in pain."

I laughed lightly. "Alas, not a fairy."

"Clemeny, I should come with you."

"I'll just go for a look around. If anything gets weird, I'll call for you. Or run like hell. Either should work."

Lionheart frowned.

"I'll take Fenton."

"That does nothing to reassure me."

"I'll be careful."

"When have you ever been careful?" Lionheart reached out and took my braid into his hand. "Call if you need me. I can hear you very well."

"Indeed, what big ears you have."

"All the better to hear you with, my dear."

"And what big eyes you have," I said, leaning toward him.

"All the better to see you with, my dear."

"And do you see me?" I whispered.

"Yes. I see you. Awake and asleep, I see you, Clemeny Louvel," he whispered then placed a soft kiss on my lips.

My body tingled from my head to my toes. I moved closer to him, wrapping my arms around him. He pulled me closer. The undeniable heat between us began to rise at once. Lionheart was beyond intoxicating. And it took every ounce of willpower within me to finally pull back.

Breathing hard, I set my forehead against his.

"Clemeny," he whispered. "Come back safe. Come back tonight. Come to me, if you will."

"I will."

He leaned forward and set a quick kiss on my lips. "Then get going."

I chuckled. "And you…go finish your business with your old friend. And just how many years have you been friends, exactly?"

"About sixty."

"That's what I guessed. And he's content to have the big, bad wolf in his house?"

"Everyone loves the big, bad wolf," Lionheart replied, smugness—but false smugness—in his voice.

"Do they?" I whispered.

"Of course. But I don't need everyone to love the big, bad wolf. I just need you. So go, and come back to me," he said then kissed me once more.

I swallowed hard then rose.

Casting one last glance at Jericho, I left the room.

I would go and be done with it. Right now, what I cared about was my future. To ensure that picture came to light, I needed to work my case, to stop the unknown assailant from ripping up London and messing up my life. Voices in the mist. Answers to riddles. They were small things. My future was in front of me. And I would do whatever I must to ensure that the life slowly piecing itself together came to fruition. But first, I needed to get my weapons.

CHAPTER 13
Back to Avalon

Taking a deep breath, I set off into the night. The ruins boasted arching towers that had once been part of the abbey walls, half-decimated buildings, broken columns, and other interesting features. One partial wall still held the shape of what must have been an ornate stained-glass window shaped like a rose. Now, only moonlight shone through the empty space. Dotted all around the grounds were apple trees, their limbs full of blossoms. The scent was heady and filled the air with its rich perfume. The smell hung in the heavy mist that enveloped the place. Jericho was right. This place did feel loose.

Of course, I knew the stories about Glastonbury Abbey. They said King Arthur and Queen Guinevere had been buried there. Given everything I knew about the oddities of the realm, I'd be stupid not to believe in the legends. At this point, I pretty much took any weird or obscure fact as truth. It saved me time. And then there were the other older, more profound myths about Glastonbury Tor. Many believed it was a gateway to the Otherworld. Or, at least, to Avalon, the enchanted land of the young and home of the mythical Lady of the Lake. Of course, those were the druids' secrets. And so far, I was hitting a wall in that regard.

As I moved through the ruins, my mind was alive, all my senses on edge. Everywhere I looked, I saw fairy globes and spirits. The place was a haunt-fest.

But the voices that always called to me were silent.

Eerily silent.

I didn't need to hear their voices.

I could feel their eyes on me.

My heart beating hard in my chest, I walked through the ruins, hunting for…well, I didn't know what.

I came to a water well. The wooden bucket rocked in the soft breeze. I stared out at the horizon. From the top of the Tor, I could see for miles. I spotted glimpses of light on the landscape, lanterns or candles in homes or on transports. I gazed into the sky overhead. Here, away from the city, there were no airships, only stars.

"Hello?" I whispered.

Nothing.

What did I expect? Did I think my long-forgotten mother would just pop out of the mists and say hi?

Yeah.

That was exactly what I expected.

I sat down at the side of the well.

And then, I waited.

And waited.

The moon crossed the sky, and it grew cold. Mist enveloped the place, and soon, the lights in the windows of Abbey House grew dim.

Wonderful.

I was getting nowhere.

Stonehenge?

Miss.

Glastonbury?

Miss.

I hoped Harper was having more luck. Gothel owed the agency a favor. If she was at Willowbrook Park, or if Miss Pendragon was able to contact Gothel, maybe Harper could find out more than me.

At this point, I was cold, thirsty, and oddly damp from all the damned fog. On the one hand, I could stay a bit more and hope something other than fairy globes passed by. Or, I could go back to the house and see what mischief Lionheart had in mind for us.

Warm and fleshy images flashed through my mind. Snuggling up beside that old werewolf would be better than sitting in the dark feeling disappointed. And cold. And dewy.

I was foolish to dream there were ever going to be any answers for me.

It was time to focus on the future and leave the past behind.

"All right, then," I said aloud to no one in particular. "I'm cold. It's late. And there is too damned much fog. Enough faerie tricks for one night. I'm done."

I headed back in the direction of Abbey House. Hopefully, Lionheart would still be awake. I imagined him sitting by the fireplace poring over some old manuscript, a glass of brandy in his hand.

I headed across the lawn toward the house, passing through the ruins once more. Using the lights in the upstairs windows of Abbey House to guide me, I made my way.

But as I walked, the lights grew dimmer.

The mist grew thicker.

The arching ruins began to fall away, replaced by a thick grove of apple trees.

I kept moving forward, but my skin had turned to gooseflesh, the palms of my hands and soles of my feet itching, my hair feeling alive with static.

I took slow, measured breaths and moved purposefully toward the lights, but the fog gathered.

Moonlight shimmered down, casting a blue glow on everything.

Ahead, I saw shapes. I moved toward them to discover they weren't ruins at all.

They were standing stones.

I swallowed hard and looked toward Abbey House. It was still here, on the horizon, where it had always been. On the horizon. But no closer.

It was still there.

But not in this world.

"Clemeny. Clemeny Louvel," a voice called from behind me.

I inhaled deeply then turned and looked.

Moonlight shimmered down on the apple trees, coloring the limbs blue, the blossoms shimmering silver in the moonlight.

Walking along a path through the apple trees and monoliths was a figure wearing a hooded robe.

My heart slammed in my chest.

"Clemeny," she said.

"Who are you?"

The woman pushed her hood back. She had long, black hair and a petite frame. "Welcome home, Clemeny."

CHAPTER 14
Can You Swim, Clemeny Louvel?

"I..." I began, but my voice faltered. A million questions raced through my mind. Inhaling slowly, I composed myself.

Remember who you are.
You are a Red Cape.
Remember why you are here.
This is about saving the Queen.
Right.
The Queen.
I'm here for Victoria.
But...
Is she my mother?
Is that my mother?
Are you my mother?

"Where am I?" I asked.

The woman extended her arm, motioning to the

trees and the stones. I spotted the long silver cuff twisting up her sleeve, the leaf pattern of the jewel sparkling in the moonlight. "You are in Avalon."

"Which is where, exactly?"

She smiled. "Not the question I expected."

"Well, I'm glad I can surprise you."

Are you my mother?

Are you my mother?

"Avalon is the world between the human world and the Otherworld. It is the guardian plane."

But are you my mother?

"I see."

The woman laughed softly and stepped closer to me. "Clemeny," she said, her expression soft. "I can hear the question on your heart."

"Then…then are you? Are you my mother?"

The woman shook her head. "No."

Unbidden and very unexpectedly, tears pricked at the corners of my eyes. "Oh."

"I am your aunt."

"My…my aunt?"

The woman nodded. "My name is Nyneve. Your mother was my sister."

"Was?" I asked, barely choking out the word.

The woman looked down for a moment. A shadow crossed her face. "Yes. My sister, your mother, is gone. But you are here now. And you've arrived just in time."

"In time for what?"

"In time to save the world."

I STARED AT THE WOMAN.

So, what to start with? My dead mother or saving the world?

"My mother…"

"The last time the world needed saving, your mother did her duty. But she died in the process. You lost a mother. I lost a sister."

"How does that land me on the steps of Saint Clement Danes?"

"Your mother was in London when everything happened. She left here pregnant and came back to us…lost. And you along with her. We know now that she gave birth to you in the city, but our enemies came for her. She hid you to keep you safe, to make you anonymous. We believe she left you at the church to hide you. For years, we didn't know what happened to you. Then, many years ago, one of us spotted you. I went to see you at Saint Clement Danes. You were with the widow Louvel. I saw that you were loved and safe. We decided it would be better for you if we left you where you were."

"Wait. Hold on. My mother left me at the church to protect me from someone who murdered her? Who?"

"The one whose dagger you're currently wearing."

I pulled the dagger from my belt. "This? Whose weapon is this?"

"His name is Melwas. He is a prince of the Unseelie Court."

"Why in the hell would he murder my mother?"

"Because she was the guardian between the worlds, the Lady of the Lake, and she would not permit him to unleash havoc on the mortal world. She died stopping him."

"Did you say Lady of the Lake?"

The woman—my aunt—nodded. "Lady of the Lake…the title is an honorific. The first Lady of the Lake, the guardian between the worlds, was a faerie. But when the faeries retreated, the Seelies left the duties of the Lady of the Lake to special humans, humans touched with sight bestowed upon them by faeries. Humans with magic in their veins. Humans like me… and you. You have the magic of Avalon in your veins. We need that magic now. We need you. Melwas is on the move. If we are to defeat him, you must take on the mantle your mother carried. The mantle of Lady of the Lake."

"I…" I began, scrunching up my brow as I tried to wrap my head around everything. "So let me get this straight. My mother stopped this Melwas from destroying the human world last time. And she died. And you all left me behind in London without ever telling me who I was or that I might be in danger. That's… fabulous. Do I have a father anywhere or…"

"Your father and mother fought together. Melwas killed them both."

"So I have two dead parents killed by a dark faerie who tried to murder *me* yesterday. And I have an aunt who left me behind as a child, not bothering to ever tell me where I came from or why I'm like this. And I've been carrying around the dagger that probably killed my own parents. And I don't even know their names."

The woman smiled gently at me. "I'm sorry, Clemeny. I know this is a lot to hear. Your mother's name was Vienne."

"And my father?"

"Your father was a Rude Mechanical. His name was Langdon."

"Langdon. Langdon Morrisey?"

"Yes. That was him."

"He was a Red Cape, not a Rude Mechanical. There is a difference."

I turned from the woman and looked toward the dim lights of Abbey House. My father had been a Red Cape. I had heard stories about him, about his dealings with the druids and other Celtic wizards in the realm.

There had been an incident twenty-three or so years ago. Not much was known about it. Most of the Red Capes in Morrisey's division died, and after that, the Rude Mechanicals shut the books on the druids and closed down the division.

My father had been a Red Cape.

And my mother was the Lady of the Lake, whatever that meant.

After a moment, I laughed.

Nyneve stepped closer to me, a confused expression on her face. "Clemeny?"

Lady of the Lake.

"Nothing. It's nothing. Just…prophets," I said, shaking my head as the Dís's words rang through my head.

Can you swim, Clemeny Louvel?

CHAPTER 15
The Druids

I looked at Nyneve. "You could have come to me. You could have told me. If you saw me, then you know what I am, what I've become. Someone could have told me something."

"Yes. We could have. But we believed Melwas would try to kill you if you were identified. You were safe with the widow Louvel."

"He tried to kill me *yesterday*."

"You *were* safe until you joined the Red Capes."

"I was never safe. I'm different. I've always had this second sight."

"It is the blood of Avalon. It is old magic. Druid magic."

"And is that what you are? A druid?"

"Yes."

"Where are the rest of you? The other druids?"

"Not far."

"You're being vague."

"Yes. And I'm sorry for it. You must understand, after my sister died, the druids retreated. We have kept our order—and ourselves—out of the world in an effort to prevent Melwas from returning."

"Looks like that plan didn't work."

"No, it did not."

"So how in the hell did he get back?"

"The stones and mounds are all guarded, shielded by druid magic. But there are ways—old, forgotten ways. We believe Melwas located an artifact that allows him to open portals to the Otherworld."

Artifact. I remembered the conversation between Victoria and the Indian agent.

"What is this artifact?" I asked.

"An amulet with three pieces. It is a device to open gateways between the worlds. The artifacts went missing many years ago."

"There was an incident with the Red Capes in India. An artifact went missing."

"Yes. It appears that the Red Capes had a piece of the artifact all along. We didn't know. After the incident with your mother and Langdon, the druids and the Rude Mechanicals ended things on bad terms."

"Did it ever occur to you that my father gave all three pieces of the artifact to the Red Capes? Maybe, in addition to telling me who I am, you could have mentioned it to me. I could have inquired. Hell, the Red Capes may have *all* the pieces. Someone should have told me something!"

"Clemeny, I know you are angry."

"No. You don't know anything. My parents are dead. For sure. For certain. I've wondered about them my whole life. And I never knew who they were or why they died. Or even that they were dead. Or why I was left behind. And I never understood why I was like this. And I didn't know I had any family, real family, still alive. And now you're here asking me to fight the same monster who killed my parents."

"Not for myself, but for the good of us all. We need your help, Clemeny. We came to you because of who you *really* are. Melwas has one piece of the artifact. This allowed him to pass through. Do you know what will happen if he gets all three pieces? All of the dark things of the Otherworld will enter the human realm. Things like the monstrous faerie Krampus whom you fought—we know about that—will enter the human plane. Melwas will become a vicious overlord, enslave mankind. It is our job to stand guard between the planes. We must stop him. I know this is hard for you. It was no easier for me. My sister was my only family. *You are my only family. I didn't want to leave you but—"*

Nyneve was interrupted when another voice called her name.

"Nyneve."

I looked behind me to find another robed figure pushing through the mist. An ancient patriarch, his long white hair and beard both drifting to his waist, approached.

I set my hand on my pistol. "Who are you?"

"My name is Elon. I am Arch Druid of the Isles. You must forgive your aunt, Clemeny. It was upon my order that we left you with Felice Louvel."

"Didn't it occur to anyone along the way—I don't know, maybe once I joined the Red Capes—to tell me who I am?"

"We are here now," Elon said.

I frowned at him. "Because you need me."

"The realm needs you, and if I am guessing correctly by that cape and badge you wear, that means something to you. I'm assuming our Queen sent you out to find answers. We're giving you the answers you seek."

He was right, but that didn't mean I wasn't still angry. "Perhaps. On the score of keeping the realm safe, you're right. But as for me, my parents, my life, you have no good excuses."

"I do have one," Elon said. "You're still alive. If

Melwas knew you lived, he would have had you killed."

"Why? It's not like I'm a druid or anything. I'm just the orphan of a woman who *was* important."

Nyneve shook her head. "No, Clemeny. You misunderstand."

"Misunderstand what?"

"Who you are. You are the Lady of the Lake, like your mother before you," Nyneve explained.

"What are you talking about?"

"You are the first daughter. The title, the power, passes on to the first daughter, as the faeries decreed generations ago. You have the magic of Avalon in your veins. We both do. But you will be Lady of the Lake, just like your mother. Only you have the power to stop Melwas."

"What? That's ridiculous. I don't have time to play around with old legends and nonsense. I have a job to do."

"We can help you, teach you," Nyneve said.

"You've had years to teach me. You chose not to. Now I have to face Melwas as I am. What I already know—not this Lady of the Lake nonsense—will have to be enough. There is no time for the rest, even though something tells me that knowing a few druid spells might have come in handy. You know, things you could have taught me *years* ago."

"She's right," Nyneve told Elon.

Elon frowned. "Melwas doesn't know who you are, why you are so strong. He knows how to fight druids, but he doesn't know how to fight you. Next time you face him, you will kill him."

"Is that so?" I asked hotly. Who in the hell was this old wizard to boss me around? I wasn't going to just start taking orders from someone who claimed to be Arch Druid. Especially not someone who had hidden the truth from me.

"Yes," Nyneve said softly. "Because if you don't, Melwas will kill Victoria and destroy everything you love," she said. Then, whispering softly under her breath, she made an odd motion with her hand.

The mists behind me parted.

I saw the ruins of Glastonbury Abbey. And then, I saw him.

Lionheart stood amongst the ruins, a sword in his hand, his eyes glowing red as he gazed all around. The moonlight shone down on him, making his blade glisten. He stilled when he spotted us.

"Clemeny?" he called.

"Track the boggarts and other dark creatures. They are working with Melwas, hunting the other two pieces of the artifact. The fiends and evil things will try to aid his rise. You must find the other two pieces of the artifact first. Get those, and you can stop Melwas from opening all the doorways into your world. The artifact Melwas has must be recovered. And you must kill him, if you can," Elon told me.

Out of the corner of my eye, I saw Lionheart moving toward us.

"What about the rest of the Unseelie? What will the Silver Court do if I murder an Unseelie prince?" I asked.

"Melwas's actions do not speak for the Silver Court. He is a rogue prince. That said, they won't raise a hand to stop him nor will they prevent you from defending this realm against him," Elon said.

Nyneve looked at me, a soft pleading expression on her face. "When it is done, sweet niece, come back. I must make amends. And you're right. You must learn."

Elon glanced behind me. "Hold, Templar. We are not your enemies."

There was a low growl behind me.

"What you ask is unfair," I told Elon. I forced myself not to tremble with the million emotions that wanted to wash over me. I felt devastated, enraged, and hopeful all at once.

"Yes," Elon said. "But that is the way of things, Lady of the Lake," he said then bowed. When he did so, the mists around him grew thick, and he disappeared.

I turned to Nyneve. "Aunt," I whispered softly.

"I'm sorry, Clemeny. I'll see you again soon," she said then vanished.

A sharp wind blew, carrying with it the heavy mist. When it passed, I found myself standing in Glastonbury Abbey ruins once more.

I looked back at Lionheart. He shook his head, tossing away the last of the wolf-like features that clung to his face. But his eyes were still glowing red.

"Are you all right?" he asked.

"Not really."

"Druids, I presume?"

"Yes."

"Did you find out what you needed to know?"

"And then some. Apparently, I'm the Lady of the Lake."

"Fancy title. Aren't you supposed to go lie in a pond and distribute swords or something?"

"That's what I thought too. But no."

"And instead?"

"I need to go kill a rogue faerie prince before he kills Victoria and lets loose havoc on our world. And, by the by, he murdered my parents."

"Sounds as though he needs a good killing." Lionheart paused. "Clemeny..."

"At least now I know why I smell good now."

"Why is that?"

"Apparently, I have the faerie-blessed blood of Avalon in my veins."

Lionheart huffed then crossed the space between us.

Wrapping his arms around me, he kissed me on the forehead. "Shall we go back and have a drink?"

"Or two."

"Or three?"

"Lead the way."

CHAPTER 16
Lions, and Lycans, and Bears, Oh My

When Lionheart and I returned to Abbey House, we stopped by the library where we found Mister Reeves asleep in his chair, a slew of papers spread out in front of him.

"Should we wake him?" I whispered.

"No need, Agent Louvel," the butler said as he entered the room behind us. "I'll see to him. May I get the two of you anything?"

Lionheart lifted a bottle and two glasses off the drink cart. "I think we're settled."

The butler chuckled. "Very well."

Lionheart motioned to me, and we headed upstairs to his room. I tiptoed to the adjoining chamber, looking in on Jericho. He was lying with his arms and legs jutting out in different directions, his mouth open wide, and his hat hanging on the bedpost. He had a sweet, peaceful look on his face.

Closing the door, I turned back to Lionheart. He'd set the cups on his dresser and was pouring us both a drink. Taking the glasses, he motioned for me to come sit beside him at the end of his bed. A fire burned in the hearth nearby, casting a cheery glow on the room.

I sat down beside Lionheart and took the cup.

"I was worried about you," he said. "I could feel something wasn't right."

"Thank you for coming for me."

"That's the first time I've been…between," he said then took a drink. "Have you ever moved between the worlds before?"

"No. But I have been close to such doorways. The druids tell me that the gates between the worlds are guarded, but this Melwas has an artifact that will allow him to enter our world."

"What does Melwas want?"

"Everything. But at the moment, he is hunting the other two parts of the artifact. Together, they create a device which opens portals to the Otherworld which will allow all the monsters to come through."

"That sounds catastrophic. I suppose we'd best head back in the morning."

"Yes," I said then took a long drink.

"Any tips on how to find him?"

"A few, but not good ones."

"Of course," he said then polished off his drink.

I finished mine as well.

Lionheart reached out for the cup. "Another?"

I shook my head.

Taking the cup from my hand, Lionheart set them on the dresser then turned back to me. Smiling softly, he stroked my hair, pushing stray strands behind my ear.

Pulling the star metal dagger from my belt, I handed it to him. "That dagger killed my parents."

Lionheart took the dagger, examined it briefly, then set it aside. "We will avenge them. Together. You are not alone anymore, Clemeny."

He slid back onto the end of the bed then pulled me into his arms.

I looked up at him.

Despite all my anger and frustration, tears began to well in my eyes. "I didn't expect…this."

"No," Lionheart said. "I'm sorry."

I nodded and brushed the hot tears from my cheeks.

"It makes me so angry. I want to punch the hell out of something."

Lionheart chuckled softly. "Remind me never to make you angry."

"You could never make me angry."

"Don't be so sure."

"I am sure. In fact, vexing as you are, you have always evoked quite the opposite emotion," I said.

Lionheart smiled softly at me. "That feeling is very mutual, Little Red."

Without thinking, I pressed my lips onto his. Both of us fell into the kiss. Months of bottled-up passion spilled over. My hands slid across his back as I slipped onto his lap. At once, I felt his want. It matched my own.

Lionheart took me by the waist and pulled us further back onto the bed.

I kissed him passionately. Feeling emboldened, I unbuttoned his waistcoat and then his shirt, pushing it off him as I drizzled kisses down his neck and chest. Part of me knew I had no business doing what I was about to do. I wasn't married. It wasn't proper. I should wait until…until what? We weren't a normal couple. I could be dead tomorrow. The faerie prince could murder me.

Lionheart slipped his hand up my blouse, stroking my back.

He moved to unbutton my shirt as I reached for the laces on his trousers.

A moment later, however, we heard a scream.

"Clemeny! Sir Richard!"

Jericho.

Half-undressed, the two of us jumped up from the

bed and raced to the adjoining bedroom. I snatched my pistol and brandished it in front of me. There, we found the boy sitting in the middle of his bed, a wild but confused expression on his face, his eyes glowing red.

"Jericho. What is it?" Lionheart asked, his voice a hard, protective snarl.

I looked at him out of the corner of my eye to see that his face had contorted somewhat into a werewolf.

My pistol raised before me, I scanned around the room.

"I...the bear...where did the man go?" Jericho asked, looking around with a baffled expression on his face.

"Bear? What man?" Lionheart asked.

Jericho looked around the room. "I had a bad dream," he said with a whimper. His mouth twisted into a hard frown, and he started crying softly.

"It's all right," I said, slipping my pistol into my trousers. I went to him. "It was just a dream."

"I dreamed that Clemeny turned into a bear, and her eyes looked like gaslamps. She was being chased by shadows. We tried to help her, but someone caught us in pens. A man was there. He was going to hurt you, Clemeny. Sir Richard, where is your shirt?"

"Oh," Lionheart said abashedly. "I was changing for...bed."

"I'm sorry. It was so scary. Will you...will you both stay with me awhile?"

I looked at Lionheart and smiled softly at him. Both of us swallowed the disappointment that was evident in our expressions.

Lionheart nodded. "Of course."

"Here, Clemeny," Jericho told me, patting one side of his bed. "And here, Sir Richard," he said, patting the other side. "Clemeny, put your pistol away, so you don't accidentally shoot yourself."

Jericho settled back down under his covers. Lionheart and I lay beside him—my pistol on the bedside table. Taking our arms, Jericho placed them over his body, our arms on top of one another.

"See. There. That's better. Now it's like we're a family," Jericho said. "I'm safe here with my family," he added then sighed and nestled down.

Lying on our sides, Jericho between us, Lionheart and I looked at one another. The weight of his words was heavy on our hearts. Very soon, Jericho fell asleep once more. His breath was deep but soft.

I stared at Lionheart. My eyes became watery, but this time, they were moved with love.

To my surprise, Lionheart's expression matched my own.

"Will you marry me, Clemeny?" he whispered.

"Yes."

"Now I just have to get Grand-mère's permission."

I giggled. "Good luck. She'll make a fuss."

"You deserve a fuss."

Jericho sighed in his sleep then whispered, "Shush."

Lionheart and I both chuckled.

"I love you," I whispered to Lionheart.

"I love you too," he whispered in reply, then slowly, the three of us drifted off into a dreamless sleep.

CHAPTER 17

Secrets, Storms, and Things that go Bump in the Night

The following morning, we packed up our things for the return trip to London.

"I'm sorry to see you go so soon," Mister Reeves told us. "I suspect this means you found what you were looking for, Agent Louvel?"

"In a fashion."

"And you, young man. I wish you well," Mister Reeves told Jericho.

"Thank you, sir," the boy replied shyly.

"Thank you for your hospitality," I said.

"Of course," Mister Reeves replied with a kind smile.

I nodded to Jericho then helped him into the car while Lionheart said goodbye.

"Mister Reeves is very nice, but I don't like this place," Jericho told me.

"No? Why not?"

"It's too high up," he said, referring to the Tor on which the house sat. "And there are too many fairies here."

I chuckled. "It is high up. And I wholeheartedly agree about the fairies. Shall we head back to London then?"

Jericho nodded. "Clemeny, why don't you live at Temple Square?"

"Because I am not part of the pack."

"Do you have to be *like us* to live there?"

"Yes."

"But I want you to come live with Sir Richard and me."

I looked at the boy. "Are you unhappy there?"

"No. It's not that. I just want you to come stay with Sir Richard and me. So we can be together. Just the three of us."

"Perhaps we'll find a way."

"I'd like that."

"Me too."

Lionheart slipped into the driver's seat. He glanced at me.

"Why are you grinning?"

"No reason."

Lionheart looked back at Jericho who was also grinning.

"I missed a good conversation," Lionheart said.

"That you did," I told him.

"Whatever the two of you are plotting, include me."

"That's the plan," I said, winking at Jericho who chuckled.

I reached across the seat and took Lionheart's hand. He smiled at me then started the steamauto, which let out a hiss.

I waved to Mister Reeves who was leaning on his cane. He nodded to me, then we drove away from Glastonbury.

As we went, I eyed the ruins. In the morning light, they were beautiful. The sunrise glowed magnificently, the sun a massive orange ball that lit up the sky with shades of tangerine and deep purple. The color cast a hue on the ruins. I knew that if I focused, I could see the world beyond, the deeper plane. But I didn't want to. Despite the fact that I was leaving Glastonbury with some of my oldest questions answered, those very answers left me feeling oddly indifferent. I couldn't change the past. My mother and father were gone. The druids told me I had some special job to do, but I had been doing that job before they decided to poke their heads out of the mist and give me a fancy title. I didn't need or want to be Lady of the Lake, as mysterious as that sounded. I was happy as I was. In fact, everything in my life was finally falling into place. I didn't need the druids to tell me to save my Queen and stop the bad guy. I'd do that on my own. Because it was the right thing to do. Because I was a Red Cape. And because protecting my world meant protecting everyone and everything I loved. And I would stop at nothing to do that.

Lionheart drove us back to Temple Square. London was very quiet. A storm had settled in over the city. The sky overhead rumbled with thunder as dark clouds rolled across the sky. There was a strange feeling in the air. I got the distinct sense that something bad was coming.

"I need to go to headquarters," I said, eyeing the sky.

Lionheart nodded. "Yes. I feel it too. I'll meet with the pack and see what's happening. When I left, Conklin was stirring up trouble."

"What's going on? Is it going to storm?" Jericho asked, looking up at the clouds.

"It may. But it will pass," I said then knelt to look him in the eyes. "In the end, it's all just water. Right?"

He nodded, but he eyed the sky skeptically.

"I'll see you soon," I said, kissing him on the forehead.

"See you soon," he replied, leaning in to hug me. He gave me a quick kiss on the cheek. "Sir Richard, I'm hungry," Jericho said, giving the sky one last skeptical glare.

"Of course you are," Lionheart said with a chuckle. "Why don't you go to the hall? I'll be there in a moment."

Jericho gave me a little wave then ran off.

Lionheart eyed the clouds then stepped closer. "Be careful," he whispered.

"You too," I replied.

We linked our hands together. "We have a lot to sort out," Lionheart said with a smile.

"At least they're good things. But it will have to wait a little while."

Lionheart nodded. "After the storm."

"After the storm."

"Please be careful."

"Always."

Lionheart shook his head then kissed me. "See you soon."

I kissed him once more then turned and headed away from Temple Square.

RM

I slipped down an alley and into the back door of a tavern called The Rusty Cog. The cook, who was preparing a ploughman's platter, looked up from his work. He nodded to me then turned back to the plate. I opened the door to a pantry and slipped inside. I stood in front of a wall of shelves lined with pickles and beets. Sliding my fingers under the uppermost ledge, I tugged on a latch. Something inside the wall clicked, and the pantry wall wagged open to reveal a narrow tunnel. I slipped inside, closing the door behind me. Crouching, I worked my way down the tight space to a small corridor at the end where a lift waited.

I slipped into the lift, closing the gate behind me, then activated the lever to lower me below the city to the waiting tram system. My thoughts turned like a whirlwind. I needed to check in with Agent Greystock to confirm what the druids had told me about the artifact. If Melwas was using this device to enter our world, then the solution to our problem was a simple one. Retrieve the device and destroy it. Or, destroy Melwas. Given what I knew now, killing Melwas seemed preferable. I also needed to find out if the other pieces of the artifact were, in fact, in the Red Capes' hands. And if so, why would the agency be foolish enough to allow such a device to exist? Perhaps they had thought that taking it to one of the colonies would protect it. My father… hadn't my father warned them? Maybe he never had a chance. Either way, it was foolish to keep the pieces of the devices in one place. Evil finds a way. Every time.

My mind also tumbled over more pleasant thoughts. Richard had asked me to marry him. And I had said yes. I had actually said yes. Without hesitation. Now what?

After. After the storm.

As the lift lowered me below the city, I started to feel the tale-tell prickle in the palms of my hands and soles of my feet. My stomach clenched. The lift came to a stop at the station, the gears overhead activating to open the doors.

On a normal day, the small tram station would be lit with gaslamps, the metal trams waiting for their riders.

But not today.

All the lights had been extinguished, and the device box to activate the tram had been smashed.

Not good.

I stayed inside the lift and debated what to do. I could just close the gate and head back up. Or…

I lowered my goggles and activated the night vision.

My senses awakened. I breathed slowly, steadily. There was someone or something not far away. Pulling my pistol, I narrowed my gaze and glanced around.

There was a strange growl, and a moment later, I spotted a pair of flashing eyes emerge from the tunnel. A beast barreled toward me. I stood frozen, staring at the monster. The creature advancing on me was mostly lion but had lizard-like scales and a menacing scorpion tail. Its face, however, was disturbingly human in its features. I had never seen anything like it.

And, of course, I was still standing in the lift carriage.

And, of course, it was headed straight toward me.

"Hell's bells."

I quickly timed the beast's movements. There was no way I could get out of the lift in time. I jumped and grabbed the pipes overhead, swinging myself up over the creature, and out onto the platform. The monster smashed head-first into the back of the lift.

I spun to face the beast. Pulling my pistol, I shot at the creature. My aim was true, but not lethal. Angered, the beast turned and pounced at me. It was incredibly fast. I quickly dashed out of the way as the monster struck at me with its tail. I dodged the strike just in time. Snarling, the creature swiped at me. I pulled my dagger and struck at the monster. My blade connected, slicing the creature, but it merely growled at me.

Dammit, what was this thing that nothing seemed to have much effect on it?

Hedging my bets, I pulled the star metal dagger. I turned and advanced on the monster, surprising it. It paused a moment then reared up on its hind legs as it prepared to launch an attack once more.

But when it did so, I struck, plunging the dagger into the beast's chest.

The monster shrieked then stiffened. A moment later, it fell over dead.

I pulled the dagger from the monster's body. A gush of blood came along with it, soaking my boots.

"Dammit."

Gripping the faerie dagger tightly, I went to the edge of the platform and jumped down onto the tracks. Pulling my pistol, I set off into the darkened tunnel toward headquarters.

CHAPTER 18
What Perseus Knew

I had just reached the line marker where another station's tram joined the main track when I heard the roar of a monster much like the one I had just killed. Everywhere was dark. All of the lamps along the line had been extinguished. I tried to track the sound of the monster in the darkness. Through my optic, I saw its shadow bounding down the ramp toward me.

I pulled the faerie dagger and made ready, but then a cold wind blew, and I heard something that sounded distinctly like…wings.

The monster yelped, and I watched in amazement as something lifted it into the air.

The beast made a strangled whining sound then dropped.

The wind whirled around me, a blur of black. A

moment later, a figure stood before me. It was the vampire, Constantine.

"I almost killed you," I said, lowering my weapon.

The fang chuckled lightly. "You'll find that hard to do."

"What are you doing here?"

"The same as you, Agent Louvel."

I raised an eyebrow at him.

"Agent Rose was headed to headquarters. I went after her only to find—"

"Lion-sized problems."

"Not lions. Manticores, Agent Louvel. Haven't you studied your mythological beasts?"

"Apparently, not well enough."

"Perhaps you're spending too much time making an *in-depth* study of the lupine kind."

I smirked. "You're one to talk. I'd be happy to trade innuendos with you, but I strongly suspect we're needed in that direction," I said, pointing down the line.

The vampire inclined his head then paused. "I could get us there a little faster if you were willing to trust me."

"Last I remember, we called things even. This will throw off the balance, won't it?

"I just saved your life. I'd say the balance is already tilted, wouldn't you?"

"I already killed a manticore on my own, thank you very much."

"You can walk if you like. I think I killed all the other manticores on this tram line, but that doesn't ensure there aren't more. Shall I go ahead and see if your colleagues are still alive?"

Annoying vampire. I didn't want to get mixed up with him again, but my heart was seized with worry. *Harper. Edwin.*

"Okay. Fine. So, what should I do?"

A split second later, the vampire was standing behind me. "Just try to relax," he said then gripped me around the waist. "You don't get motion sick, do you?"

Before I could answer, he blasted into the air with such outrageous speed that I could barely keep my wits about me. We shot down the tunnel. As we went, I saw that all of the stations had gone dim. A few moments later, we arrived at the tram station situated just below headquarters. With a whoosh, the vampire alighted and set me down.

It took me a moment to catch my breath.

Everything was eerily silent.

There was a massive smear of blood on the floor. The lift carriage was missing.

"Stairs?" I asked, pointing.

Constantine frowned as he stared at the lift shaft then cursed…in Latin.

Moving quickly, he grabbed me by the waist once more then we flew up the lift shaft to the nearest floor which housed Artifacts and Archives and Tech. The door to the shaft was open. The vampire alighted just inside.

This time, I almost threw up.

I swallowed hard then looked all around.

Everything was dark. There was an alarm ringing throughout the building.

The vampire stilled, his eyes shimmering silver in the darkness. "Aurora isn't here. I'm going up to the next level. Would you like…"

I shook my head. "No."

He nodded, and without another word, disappeared into the dark shaft once more.

I pulled the faerie dagger and my pistol and headed off in the direction of Artifacts and Archives. Headquarters was a repository for information. All that paperwork meant that headquarters had lots of records but not much in the way of security. Most Red Capes were field agents. If someone attacked headquarters, they would find little resistance. Everyone would have been vulnerable.

I turned the corner to discover my first body.

The lights in the corridor leading to archives were only half-extinguished. A junior agent, someone I recognized only by her face, lay slumped on the floor in a puddle of blood. Kneeling, I checked for a pulse.

Nothing.

Anger boiled up in me.

Gripping the dagger hard, I rushed down the hallway. When I reached the end, I saw the lamps in the Artifacts room glowing. Inside, I heard someone cursing under their breath and the sound of crates being pushed to the floor.

I slid close to the door and listened.

From what I could hear, there was only one person in the room. But who? If it was Melwas, I needed to be ready.

I stared ahead of me, trying to think about what to do, when I noticed a shield displayed on the wall there.

Greek monsters.

Not a bad idea, vampire.

I carefully lifted the shield off the wall then slid as close to the door as I could. Angling the inside of the polished shield as best I could, I pulled off Perseus's move on Medusa. Looking at the reflection, I spotted a single figure at the back of the room sifting through boxes. It wasn't Melwas. I winced when some ancient-looking artifact hit the floor and shattered into a million pieces. Tilting the shield, I searched the room for signs of any monsters. Nothing.

Moving carefully, I set the shield down. Bending

low, I crept into the room and down the aisle opposite the man.

"Bloody hell," the stranger said, tumbling another box onto the floor. "Where the hell is it?"

Taking my chance, I rounded the corner and grabbed the creature, putting the faerie blade to the man's neck.

"So, what are you looking for?"

"What the—"

"No chatter. I asked you a question."

"None of your business, Red Cape," he hissed. I felt a strange buzz in the air. A moment later, the brute of a man I was holding shifted. Slipping out of my arms, he changed shape into that of a slim young man. He slid out of my grasp. Turning, he pulled a pistol on me.

"No," I screamed but ducked all the same, diving behind some boxes just as the boggart took a shot.

He missed.

"You don't have to die, boggart. Just tell me what you're looking for," I called, tracking the man's feet under the table.

As I went, I noticed a crumpled figure lying under a heap of boxes.

Agent Greystock.

Gasping, I reached out and touched her wrist. I didn't see any sign of blood, but she wasn't moving. There were terrible black-and-blue marks on her temple. She was still alive. Unconscious, but alive.

Feeling my fury boil up in me, I tracked the boggart down the length of the room.

"I have no intentions of dying, Red Cape. And I'm not telling you anything," he said, then he lowered himself and took a shot at me.

Expecting the move, I heaved myself quickly onto the table, up and over the boxes, then jumped onto the shapeshifter. I could feel the energy around us gather, but this time, I was ready. Grabbing my silver cuffs, I slapped the first on his wrist.

The boggart howled then twisted in an effort to get away. But wrestling with a half-shifted boy was nothing compared to wrestling a werewolf. In no time, I had the other cuff on him. Bound in silver, there was no way he could escape.

Unless, of course, he tried to run.

Which he did.

Hell's bells.

Dashing out of the Artifacts room, he raced down the hallway. I hurried after him. Aiming my pistol, I took a shot. I missed when he slipped in the puddle of blood at the end of the hall and went tumbling sideways.

I raced after him in time to see him slip toward the open lift entrance.

"Shite," I cursed through clenched teeth then dove

after him, catching him by the collar of his shirt just as he slid through the open edifice.

Bracing my foot against the wall, I pulled him back. But then I thought better of it. Tightening my grip, I paused, holding the boggart precariously on the ledge.

"Pull me up. Now, dammit!"

I clicked my tongue at him. "What were you looking for?"

"None of your business."

"You know I could drop you, right?" In fact, despite the fact that the boggart had shifted form into a youth, he was still exceedingly heavy. Very soon, I would have to either pull him up—with or without answers—or drop him.

He was silent for a moment.

"Come on. I know Melwas sent you. What are you looking for?"

"He'll kill me."

"I'll kill you. That's an agent lying dead on the floor back there. And another one in the room unconscious."

"That wasn't me! That was Melwas. He tore up the place then left me down here."

"Where is he?"

"I don't know. He went upstairs."

"What are you looking for?"

"I...an artifact."

"Obviously." Dammit, he was getting heavy. "You're

being less than specific, and this shirt is clearly not bespoke. Stitches are ripping. Better talk faster."

"You'll pull me up if I talk?"

"That's my plan."

"You… I know who you are. You're Little Red, aren't you? The werewolf hunter."

"Why?"

"You give me your word that you'll pull me up. If I have your word, I'll talk."

"You have my word," I said then with a heave, tugged him back over the edge.

He slid toward the wall.

"Well?"

"In my pocket," he said, looking down toward his shirt pocket.

Reaching forward, I pulled out a piece of paper. There, I saw a sketch of an odd-looking device with a clockwork base, a narrow shaft, and a gemstone cap. "He's after the shaft and the stone. He has the tuning device."

"And he thinks they're here?"

"He knows they're here."

"Why are you working for him? Do you know what he's planning?"

"I do, but he's paying in faerie metal, Agent. Do you know how rare that is? It's a big world. I don't need to stay in England."

"Wonderful, so you'll let him destroy us all while you run away. All of this is assuming he doesn't kill you rather than paying you."

The boggart frowned but said nothing.

Sighing, I grabbed the boggart by his cuffs and pulled him toward the wall. Snatching the flail mace that had been displayed on the wall, I wrapped the chain around his cuffs then wedged the handle behind some pipes, rendering the boggart immobile.

"What in the hell are you doing?" he demanded.

"I kept my promise and didn't drop you. You kept your promise and told me the truth. Now I need to go deal with Melwas."

"You need to let me go."

"That wasn't part of the deal."

"If Melwas finds me, he'll kill me."

"Not if I kill him first."

"You can try, Agent. But you will fail."

"That's what they told me about Fenton, and now he makes a nice accessory."

"Melwas isn't like *us*," he said, staring me in the eyes. "He's powerful, strong."

"Well then, I guess I'll just have to outsmart him. As for you, I can't have you going anywhere. Sorry about this," I said. Lifting my pistol, I struck the boggart hard, rendering him unconscious.

Turning, I rushed back to the artifact room where Agent Greystock lay unconscious.

"Agent Greystock," I called, rushing to her. I knelt before her and shook her shoulder. "Eliza," I said, shaking her once more.

A whimper escaped her lips.

"Agent Greystock," I said again.

"Clemeny?"

"I'm here. You got knocked out."

She groaned.

"Eliza?"

"I think my arm is broken," she whispered. She was half-unconscious.

"The entire place is under attack. They're looking for the artifact. Is it here?"

"Upstairs. Hunter."

I rose. "Stay here. Stay quiet. I'll stop Melwas then come back for you. There are monsters in the building. Stay quiet. Do you hear me, Eliza?"

"Quiet," she whispered then drifted off again.

Hell's bells!

I rushed out of the room, closing the door behind me in the simple hope it would be enough to keep her safe from any manticores lurking.

As for me, I was headed upstairs after a different monster.

There was no way Melwas was getting out of there alive.

CHAPTER 19
Workroom Blitz

I rushed up the steps to the next level, Records, which was entirely silent. I knew that Constantine was somewhere. And, I hoped, Agent Rose. Something told me that if anything happened to her, the vampire might start a war with the entire Unseelie race. Not a warming prospect. I slipped down a hallway and into the narrow passage that led up to a servant's entrance to the main workroom.

As I neared the top steps, I heard shouting. Then shooting.

"There, over there," Harper screamed.

The sound of terror in her voice made my blood run cold.

I opened the door a crack.

Everywhere was dark, but I heard the tell-tale growl of the manticore—or manticores. The room was black, the lamps extinguished. I could smell the scent of lamp oil in the air. I could see some agents moving in the brief snatches of light as gunshots were fired. And when I did so, I saw bodies on the floor, including Agent Martin Fox. Clenching my jaw, I pulled on my night optic goggles.

"Harper, look out," I heard Hank call followed by gunshots.

Grasping the faerie dagger in one hand, my pistol in the other, I kicked open the door.

The first of the manticores spotted me. Distracted by the noise and the glow of my night optics, it turned toward me.

"Everyone get down," I said then started shooting.

The monster wasted no time. He rushed across the desktops then leaped toward me. I hoisted a chair and bashed the monster to the side. Dazed, he struggled to get up. I moved fast, the star metal dagger glowing, then slit the beast's throat.

"Clemeny, another one," someone called. Was it Cressida?

I heard grunting and the sound of breaking glass as another monster rushed me. Dammit, this one was bigger than the others. And it had wings.

The monster jumped off the table and pounced at me. I slashed with the dagger, but not before the beast caught me with his claws. The sharp nails raked my arm. I gasped but swallowed my scream. He knocked me to the ground. Surprised, it took me a moment to regain my senses, which I did just seconds before the scorpion-like tail whipped at me.

"Here, here," Harper called, and something came hurtling at the monster.

Was that a coat rack?

Her move distracted the beast long enough for me to get to my feet.

"Clemeny, move," Agent Keung called from somewhere in the darkness. A moment later, I spotted the agent rushing across the desktops, a sword in hand. He slashed at the monster's tail, but the beast's back leg shot out, batting him away before he could swipe. Agent Keung flew back and hit the wall hard.

It was my chance. I raced forward then plunged the dagger deep into the monster's eye.

It let out a great howl.

Its tail struck at me, a last ditch effort to take me out, but the beast was weakening.

I moved back, nearly tripping over the scattered pieces of broken furniture on the floor. The monster tried to knock the weapon out of its eye, but it was too late. The manticore crumpled to the floor a moment later.

Across the room, someone struck a match.

"Careful. There is lamp oil everywhere," Hank said.

Cressida lifted a lamp. The orange light illuminated her face with weird shadows. Blood trickled down her cheek. Though the place was dimly lit, I could see that the agency workroom had been destroyed.

Panic on her face, Harper looked from me then scanned the room.

"Edwin?" she called. She rushed toward a heap of overturned desks. "Edwin? Edwin," she called pushing the broken furniture aside. "Someone help me."

There were five of us still standing. Other agents lay dead or unconscious on the floor. Hank, Cressida, Agent Keung and I rushed to help Harper.

"Where is Melwas?" I asked as I started moving broken furniture.

"We haven't seen anyone. Just the manticores," Agent Keung replied.

"What about Agent Rose?" I asked.

"Haven't seen her," Cressida answered.

We slowly lifted an overturned desk. There, we found a badly bruised and bloodied Agent Hunter. My heart skipped a beat.

"Agent Hunter," Hank called.

He didn't answer.

Harper pushed the remaining debris furniture away. "Edwin? Edwin," Harper called, shaking his shoulder gently.

I stared at her. *Could it be?*

Harper set her head on his chest. She listened for a moment. "He's alive," she said with a huge sigh.

"Elaine?" Edwin whispered softly.

"I'm here," Harper replied, taking Edwin's hand.

Well, well, well.

I saw Cressida look at me, but I didn't meet her gaze.

Dipping into my vest pocket, I grabbed a scarf. The manticore scratch stung like hell. I quickly wrapped my arm.

From the back of the station, I heard a crash.

"Clemeny," Agent Keung said warningly.

"Go upstairs. Make sure the townhouse agents are safe. We need to send an alert. All field agents must meet at the secondary station at once. We're in trouble. We also need to get an airship aloft. Send a messenger to Willowbrook Park. Call the Pellinores...and Miss Pendragon," I said then turned to Harper. "Harper, did you find Gothel?"

She didn't answer. She merely held Edwin's hand.

"Harper," I said again, my voice sharp.

"Clemeny?" She looked up at me, a confused and guilty expression on her face. There was no time for that. Whatever had blossomed to life between Edwin and Harper since the incident at Cabell Manor didn't matter—*much, or at least, I couldn't think about it right now.*

"At Willowbrook Park, did you find Gothel?" I repeated my voice sharp.

She shook her head. "No, but Rapunzel was going to try to contact her."

"We need the Pellinores," I told the others.

Hank huffed, half-laughing. "Why?"

"Because if we are going to do battle for this realm, I want the only living descendant of King Arthur front and center. And she is with the Pellinores," I said, then turned back to Agent Keung. "Make sure Miss Pendragon is on that airship."

He nodded.

The Pellinore division had been the butt of a running joke in our office. Their division monitored dragon bloods, descendants of Mordred, bastard son of King Arthur. Most people thought that being a Pellinore amounted to babysitting a handful of thugs. But last summer, the Pellinores uncovered a dragon caller, Rapunzel, a true heir of King Arthur, and her faerie guardian, Gothel. Her arrival was ominous. I should have known that old blood was stirring and something big was on the horizon. But like everyone else, I also discounted the Pellinores. Now, however, I was beginning to see how all the pieces of the puzzle fell together.

I turned to Hank and Cressida. "Agent Greystock is in Artifacts. She's hurt. Other agents have been…killed. You'll find a boggart tied up down there. Agent Rose and Constantine are around here somewhere. And Melwas."

"Is it true? An Unseelie Prince?" Cressida asked.

I nodded. "I think I'll go find him and have a little chat."

"Clemeny," Edwin whispered, motioning for me to come close.

I knelt beside him. "Don't try to talk. Just rest."

"No," he said. "My office. Inside Tinker's Tower. On my desk. He can't find it."

I nodded. Whatever we Red Capes had been hiding, Melwas was dangerously close to uncovering it.

"I'll take care of it," I reassured Edwin then turned to Harper.

"I should come," she said.

I shook my head then set my hand on Harper's shoulder. "Take care of him," I said then rose.

That faerie was going to pay.

CHAPTER 20
Your Friendly Neighborhood Vampire

I took a deep breath then turned and headed in the direction of Edwin's office.

Fully aware that there could be other boggarts or manticores lurking abound, I allowed my senses to work overtime. I was filled with so much rage it made my hands tremble. I tried not to think about the fact that my colleagues were dead, that my friends were hurt, and that my agency was blitzed. On top of that, this piece of rubbish had gone after my Queen.

And, if what the druids said was true, he had killed my parents.

I pulled off my goggles and stuck them in my pocket.

I breathed in slowly, in and out, then opened my eyes.

And this time, I let myself see. Really see. I scanned

the hallway, the sight in my mooneye amplified. I could see our world and the spirit world overlapping.

"The Lady of the Lake is the guardian between the worlds."

Or, she had excellent eyesight. I wasn't sure I had bought this whole Lady of the Lake bit. Until I started controlling water or pulling magical swords out of mud puddles, I wasn't buying it. But the idea that there was some magical blood in me made a little sense. It would explain…a lot. At least it explained why my boyfriend —no, fiancé—thought I smelled so good.

From the direction of Edwin's office, I heard something crash.

I moved toward the noise.

Toward the danger.

Always toward the danger.

One of these days, it was going to get me killed.

There was a very dim light burning in the room.

Steeling my nerve, I stepped toward the door, but someone grabbed my arm.

I turned around.

A pair of flashing silver eyes looked back at me.

Agent Rose.

"Wait," she mouthed soundlessly.

She tilted her head and motioned for me to step into one of the other offices with her. The room was pitch black, but I spotted the shape of Constantine in the shadows. He stepped forward, almost like he was emerging from the shadows themselves.

"He has a beast in the room with him," Constantine whispered.

"There is something in that room we need to get to before he finds it."

"What is it?" Agent Rose asked.

"A magical artifact."

Agent Rose sighed. "And of course it's right there. Fine. I'll take the beast, the two of you go for the faerie."

Constantine nodded to her.

"Are you sure?" I asked, surprised.

She winked at me, her eyes sparkling. "Trust me."

"Lure him out," Constantine told me. "Lead him to the lift shaft."

"And when I get to the lift shaft?"

"Jump."

"Jump?"

"I'll catch you."

I shook my head. Fangs. "All right."

With that, we moved toward the door. Constantine melded into the shadows once more then disappeared down the hallway. I signaled to Rose. Through the narrow crack in the door, I could make out Melwas. And the manticore. I had always admired Edwin's office until now. Now it was a little cramped for hand-to-hand combat. I scanned the room. The small replica of Tinker's Tower that sat on Edwin's desk was undisturbed. Agent Rose moved toward the door, but the floorboard below her foot squeaked. Melwas and the manticore looked at her.

"Oops," she said with a wicked grin.

The manticore growled.

"Kill her," Melwas commanded.

Moving faster than I thought possible, Rose rushed down the hallway in the other direction, the monster bounding after her.

I waited a breath then turned and entered the room.

Melwas, who had been rifling through a cabinet, stopped cold. He turned and looked at me, his eyes glimmering. He looked me over from head to toe, his gaze resting on the faerie dagger stuffed into my belt.

"That's mine," he said.

"Why don't you come take it from me?"

The faerie smirked. "Overbold, Agent," he said then rushed me.

I turned and ran from the office, down the hall toward the lift shaft.

The faerie cursed.

A moment later, I felt the energy around me charge. Magic filled the air. Glancing over my shoulder, I saw that Melwas had stopped. He was twisting his hands in a ball, forming a glowing blue light, which, no doubt, he was going to blast at me.

Hell's bells.

I couldn't wait to go back to fighting werewolves.

I grabbed an ornamental spear off the wall and hurled it toward him, wincing in pain as the movement aggravated the scratch on my arm.

Not expecting the move, the faerie broke off his spell just in time to get out of the way. The blade on the long spear sliced his shoulder. The steel burned him. He hissed in pain then turned and glared at me.

"You're really starting to get on my nerves," he growled.

"You started it," I said then slowly began to back toward the lift shaft.

I really, really, really hoped Constantine was planning to keep his word.

The faerie rushed me again. I ran to the lift. The door was open; the lift was on the floor above us. The shaft from here to the tram level was empty. I jumped, grabbing onto the shaft cables.

The faerie reached the opening then stared at me.

Saying a silent prayer, I linked my arms and legs around the cable then began my quick slip downward. I looked up only to see the faerie glaring at me. Frustrated, he leaped into the shaft, leapfrogging back and forth along the tunnel walls.

Hell's bells. He was catching up quickly.

I glanced down. The bottom of the tunnel was fast approaching.

"Any time now," I called into the darkness.

There was a rush of cold air then a moment later, a colony of bats surrounded me. The sight was slightly terrifying. From amongst the bats, the handsome face of the vampire Constantine appeared.

"What took you so long?" I said.

The vampire grinned then grabbed me by the waist, lowering me quickly to the ground.

We landed softly then looked up, waiting as the faerie neared us.

"And do we have a plan for when he gets here?" I whispered.

"If he doesn't cooperate, I could just eat him," Constantine suggested.

"Might give you an upset stomach."

"That's what I was thinking. Perhaps that dagger will work better."

Melwas landed on the ground before us, his cloak swirling around him. He righted himself then let out a long, low whistle which reverberated down the narrow tunnel, echoing in the darkness. From somewhere not far away, a series of howls answered him.

But they were not the howls of a manticore.

I knew that sound very well.

Somewhere in the darkness was a pack of wolves.

"Shite," I whispered.

The faerie looked from me to Constantine.

"You're on the wrong side of this battle, fiend," Melwas told Constantine.

"You're not the first tyrant to tell me something like that," the vampire replied.

"Then you must be very stupid if you haven't learned by now."

Constantine's rage rolled from him with such force that the air shuddered. A moment later, he disappeared into the shadows.

"Darkness has come for the light. You've picked a fight with the gods, Agent Louvel," Melwas hissed at me.

"I've met gods before. You are no god," I said. "And you should call me Little Red," I said then pulled the faerie dagger and attacked.

CHAPTER 21
Just One Damned Monster After Another

My first go around with the faerie taught me he was fast—faster than anything I had ever fought before. But then, I hadn't known he was the one who had killed my parents. Now, I knew. Now, I had a reason.

With a twirl, the faerie attacked, landing a solid hit to my jaw.

I staggered backward. The faerie struck once more, kicking at my arm, trying to disarm the dagger. If he thought he was going to take that from me, he was horribly mistaken. I grabbed the faerie's leg and yanked hard, pulling him off his feet.

The sound of howls grew louder.

Now I was twice as mad. Someone had turned on the Templars. Who?

I heaved up the dagger, moving to stab the bastard,

but he rolled out of the way. As Melwas leaped back, he was swept up by a torrent of bats and slammed against the wall.

The vampire dropped the faerie to the ground then looked over his shoulder at me.

I had seen Constantine's true vampire face once before when Agent Rose's life had been threatened. All teeth and malice, it was a horrifying sight.

"Louvel," he said, motioning behind me.

I looked back to see three werewolves emerge from the shadows.

Conklin.

Of course.

While the Templars had crushed the old packs into submission or sent them abroad, the tension with the packs that had been loyal to Cyril and Fenton was always right below the surface. Before me was proof of that. A ragtag group of barely mature wolves, what was left of the Conklin pack, was made up of werewolves who were probably no older than me. They had begrudgingly sworn allegiance to the Templars. Apparently, they hoped Melwas would turn their luck around.

With a sigh, I slipped the star metal dagger into its holster then pulled my pistol and silver.

"Really, Acwellen," I said to their leader, a young wolf with ebony-colored fur. "Aligning with the Unseelie? You know that pompous bastard just sees you as some damned dumb mutt he can use to—oh, I don't know—distract me from killing him."

I cast a glance over my shoulder. From the looks of things, there might not be a lot left of Melwas to kill once Constantine was done with him.

"We have our own reasons to be here, Louvel. That's my daddy hanging off your belt," Acwellen replied.

"Yeah, I suppose that would piss me off too. But Fenton did try to kill me and mine. And I offered to let him live."

"You're lying."

"Am I?"

The werewolf glanced at the others. If he had half a brain, he could guess I was telling the truth.

But he didn't.

He turned back to me, his red eyes glowing. He growled low and mean.

"No? Not ready for the truth? Might as well come at me then," I said then raised my pistol.

And with a growl, that was precisely what he did.

More frustrated than angry, I went after the wolves. They were standing between Melwas and me. Acwellen pounced at me in the darkness. I dodged quickly to the side, rushing up the curved tunnel wall then jumped, shooting as I did so. My first bullet was a miss, but the second shot hit another of the wolves who yelped then fell to the ground.

Acwellen rushed forward. Taking a swipe, he slapped my wounded arm, knocking my pistol from my hand. I winced then brandished my blade before me, slicing the wolf.

The blade caught his cheek, ripping a long slash.

The werewolf jumped back.

The third of the motley pack lunged at me, his red eyes widening when he saw—

far too late—me crouch. I lifted the blade over my head and held on. The dagger made contact, slicing the wolf's belly wide open. He hit the wall with a hard thud then slid to the ground, immobile.

I rose. With two of the wolves dispatched, that only left Acwellen.

The wolf moved to attack once more, but then a raven flew overhead, squawking loudly. The random appearance of the bird distracted the wolf. He paused. A moment later, Agent Rose appeared. She leapt onto the back of the wolf.

"Louvel," she called, her arm outstretched.

I tossed my dagger.

Agent Rose caught it with perfect accuracy then plunged it into the werewolf's neck.

The creature let out a half-howl then collapsed.

Rose leaped off.

The two of us turned and, together, moved toward Constantine and Melwas.

For a brief moment, the two broke apart. Constantine stepped back. He looked over his shoulder at what was left of the wolves then again at the faerie who was panting hard.

"You'll have to try harder than that," I told the faerie.

Melwas said nothing. He looked at the three of us then began to slowly step back.

But there was nowhere to go.

Unless…

The darkness gathered around him, and he began speaking in a low tone. He was holding something in his hands. The device.

"Another day…Little Red," he said.

Then, I caught that strange earthy scent once more.

"No," I yelled, rushing forward. But it was too late. A greenish light shimmered, showing the outline of the faerie, and then he was gone.

"Dammit!"

"At least he didn't get what he was after," Agent Rose said.

I stared into the darkness where the faerie had been.

No. He hadn't. But he would be back. And next time, he wasn't going to get away so easily.

CHAPTER 22
Bloody Boggarts

Agent Rose, Constantine, and I returned upstairs to the workroom which had been relit. I inhaled slowly and deeply, taking in the destruction. The faerie and his lackeys had destroyed Headquarters.

Agent White and Agent Jones were directing the medics who were taking the wounded agents upstairs.

"I'll meet you later," Constantine whispered to Agent Rose.

I looked back at the vampire who nodded to me, then he melded into the shadows and disappeared.

"Agent White," I called, joining the junior agent. She had a smear of blood on her chin and was sweating. "Where did they take Agent Hunter and Agent Greystock?"

"We got word to Her Majesty. The wounded are

being transported to Buckingham. In fact, there was a message for you. Oh, here he comes…" she said then looked to the lift.

When the lift doors opened, Agent Martin Fox stepped out.

Without a scratch on him.

"Agent Louvel," he called. "There you are. I have an urgent message for you from Her Majesty."

My eyes scanned the floor. I had seen Agent Fox, seen him lying dead not far from where Edwin had been. When I looked now, there was nothing. Had I been mistaken? Had it been someone else?

I rushed across the room quickly and grabbed Agent Fox. Pulling my spare silver cuffs off the back of my belt, I slapped them on him.

"What? Clemeny, what in the hell are you doing?"

"Hell's Bells," I said then turned to Agent Rose. "I saw Agent Fox dead. There," I said, pointing. "It must have been—"

"A boggart," Agent Rose finished for me.

I could feel all the color drain from my face. If that had been a boggart, then he would have heard what Edwin had told me.

Turning, I raced down the hallway toward Agent Hunter's office.

"Clemeny, I need your key. Clemeny? You gotta let

me out of these cuffs," Agent Fox—the real Agent Fox —called.

I knew even before I got there.

I knew.

I turned the corner into Edwin's office to see the replica of Tinker's Tower smashed open. Picking up the remaining pieces, I looked inside.

From my periphery, I spotted Agent Rose at the door.

"Gone," I told her, dropping the piece onto Hunter's desk.

"The faerie got what he wanted."

I nodded ruefully.

"Now what?"

"Clemeny," Agent Fox called, joining Agent Rose and me in Edwin's office. "Christ, they tore the place up. What were they looking for?"

"Something that they found," I said with a sigh.

"Clemeny, Her Majesty wants you to come to Buckingham at once."

"I'm sure she does."

Agent Rose raised an eyebrow at me.

"The faerie is reconstructing a device. It contains three pieces. Once he has all three, he can open all the doorways to the dark fey realm."

"And how many pieces does he have now?" Agent Rose asked.

"Two."

"And the third?"

I shook my head as I scanned the room. My eyes fell on a painting of Victoria hanging on the wall. I studied it closely then huffed a laugh.

"It's hanging off our Queen's neck."

CHAPTER 23
What the Queen and King Said

A gent Rose and I followed a palace guard down the winding halls of Buckingham, deeper and deeper into the castle.

"Ever been here before?" I asked Agent Rose.

An odd little smile came to her face. "Yes. Long ago."

The guard stopped at the door then signaled for Agent Rose and me to wait.

Agent Rose studied me. "You ought to have someone look at that arm."

"Yeah. Afterward."

"You know how this goes. There is no afterward."

The door opened. "Come," the guard said, motioning for the two of us to come inside.

Her Majesty was sitting at a desk. The room was dimly lit, a fireplace casting the light.

The Queen shuffled some papers. "So, he destroyed my museum and has now destroyed the Red Cape headquarters. I understand you gave the order to call all the agents to the tower, Agent Louvel?"

"Yes, Your Majesty."

"On whose authority?"

Shite. "Um, I just thought we needed to rally, Your Majesty. Somewhere safe."

"I see. And you've also called the Pellinores and Miss Pendragon to London?"

"Yes, Your Majesty."

"Well, Agent Louvel, seems you've placed yourself in charge of the Red Capes…"

"Your Majesty, forgive me, I—"

"No, no," she interrupted. "I was planning to promote you to director anyway. Edwin is going to take over in India. I simply hadn't had the opportunity to inform you of the promotion," she said then rose, coming around the back of her desk.

She gazed at Agent Rose. "Aurora."

"Your Majesty," Agent Rose said, curtseying lightly.

Her Majesty rolled her eyes then turned back to me. "I assume this means you have some semblance of a plan in the works."

"I'm getting there, but I have a complicated problem," I said.

"And that is?"

"That," I said, pointing to the faerie gemstone hanging from the Queen's neck.

"Has he found the other pieces?"

"Yes."

"Then I suppose he'll be after my neck now," she said. "Quite literally."

"Why don't you give it to Louvel?" Agent Rose suggested.

"The faerie jewel?"

Agent Rose shrugged. "Put it on Louvel. Let them see she has it, and they'll leave you alone."

"If Melwas realizes you have the stone, he'll come for you. But if I have it…" I said.

"Putting the stone on you and sending you after Melwas brings two things together that should be kept far, far apart," Queen Victoria said.

"True," Agent Rose interjected. "But it will save your life."

"Unless Louvel dies," the Queen replied.

"Are you planning on dying?" Agent Rose asked me pertly.

"Not today. I just got promoted," I said with a grin.

Queen Victoria looked from Agent Rose to me. With a sigh, she pulled off the massive blue-green gem then handed it to me. When the stone touched my open palm, it glowed bright blue.

I stared at the gem. Not only did it glow blue, but I

could have sworn it was beating like a heart. I felt a strange thumping in my hand. The blue light emanating from the stone lit the room.

"Curious," Queen Victoria said. "Who is your family, Agent Louvel?"

"The answer to that is rather complicated," I replied. I slipped the necklace on. The light dimmed when it lay on my breastplate but didn't entirely extinguish.

"Well, that should get Melwas's attention," Agent Rose said.

"I think it would be best if Your Majesty moved to a safe location," I told Victoria.

"I'm sure you think so, Agent, but I'm not going anywhere. You aren't the only one who is willful and stubborn."

"You're the Queen. You may be as willful and stubborn as you like."

At that, Victoria chuckled lightly. "So I shall. The wounded agents are in the west wing of the palace. I understand Agent Harper is there."

"She should be, Your Majesty."

"Send her along. She will see to the security detail for myself and my family. Once you rendezvous with the Red Capes at the tower, dispatch additional agents here."

"Of course, Your Majesty."

"And I hope you have an excellent reason for calling

in Miss Pendragon. You don't hope to depose me in the midst of all of this, do you, Louvel?"

"Your Majesty, I am loyal to—"

Her Majesty laughed lightly. "Of course. But why have you asked for Miss Pendragon?"

"Who is Miss Pendr—" Agent Rose began, but Queen Victoria raised a hand to silence her.

"I don't know why, exactly. Just…instinct," I said.

Queen Victoria cocked her head as she thought it over. "Instinct. Very well. Now, go kill this bloody faerie so I can get back to business. And don't lose my necklace," the Queen said then waved us away.

I nodded to Agent Rose, and we headed out of the chamber.

Agent Rose and I turned and headed toward the west wing of the castle.

"So, who is Miss Pendragon?"

"A dragon blood. No, that's not right, a dragon caller."

Agent Rose scrunched up her forehead as she considered my words. To my surprise, she made no jests about the Pellinores. "Pendragon?"

"Descendant of King Arthur."

"A real heir?"

"Yes."

"No wonder Vikki has her knickers in a twist," Agent Rose said with a laugh.

I stared at her. What in the world had transpired between the two of them that had led to such...tension?

"Sorry, Louvel. I forgot you were such a royalist."

"And you aren't?"

"Depends on the monarch."

We wound down the narrow stairs until we reached the chamber in which at least a dozen Red Capes were receiving medical care. Agent Greystock lay in her bed, a massive bandage on her forehead, her arm wrapped. Harper was sitting at Edwin's bedside.

Agent Rose glanced at me. "Shall I go give Harper the news?"

I nodded. "Yeah, thanks." Whenever Harper and I did have a chance to talk, it was going to be awkward, and right now, I had no time for awkward.

Crossing the room, I went to Agent Greystock. I pulled up a chair beside her. She opened her eyes a crack and looked at me.

"Well, he didn't get you yet," she said with a half-smile. "Too tough to kill, I suppose."

"That makes two of us," I replied.

She looked me over, eyeing the pendant hanging on my neck. "She gave it to you."

I nodded. "I'm the bait now."

"Considering how badly he wants it, don't think for a moment he won't take your head to get it. It's a bit more *luminescent* than I remember."

"So it is. Have any thoughts on that?"

"A few."

"I went to Glastonbury. Met some people there. I was wondering, given your friendship with Grand-mère, if you ever did a little poking around. Maybe in Glastonbury. Maybe in the agency records."

Agent Greystock studied my face. "I might have. I love Felice. And you. What I might have discovered wouldn't have helped anyone."

"What did you discover?"

"That you are an orphan, which you already know."

"And?"

"And...the rest seemed like fairy tales."

"But isn't that our business? Fairy tales?"

"That depends. Some people don't want to be wrapped up in fairy tales. Some people carve their own paths, make their own way. They don't need fairy tales to be extraordinary. What little I discovered...I'm not sure it would have helped you. I hope you understand my meaning. And if not, I hope you will forgive me."

I did understand her. What did knowing about my parents and the link to Avalon really matter? In the end, I was still doing my job just like I would have anyway. I didn't need a myth to define who I was. I was who I was because of people like Grand-mère and Quinn and Agent Greystock. Not because, once upon a time, my family line—*which I knew nothing about*—had been charged with some sacred duty. All it had ever done for me thus far was make me smell good. I had guided my own path thus far. And I was proud of what I had accomplished. Hell, Queen Victoria had just made me the new director of the Red Capes.

"I do," I said then set my hand on her shoulder. "You should rest."

"And you should have someone look at that arm."

I nodded. She was right.

Exchanging one last glance with Agent Greystock, I rose and crossed the room to join one of the doctors. "Have a minute?" I asked.

He looked up at me.

I pointed to the bloody scarf around my arm. "Probably just a flesh wound, but just in case."

"What got into you?"

"Same as this lot."

"Sit," he said then unwrapped the bloody gauze, motioning for me to pull off my coat. I was surprised how much it hurt to remove the sleeve.

The doctor frowned at the wound. He poured some fresh water into a basin then began cleaning me up. The scratches, made from four razor-sharp talons, were swollen and achy.

"This will hurt a bit," he said then dabbed on some alcohol.

I gritted my teeth. "A bit?"

"Sorry. I lied. I meant a lot."

Grabbing a blue jar full of strangely stinky salve, he liberally applied the ointment to the wound. When he was done, he wrapped my arm with a clean bandage.

"I am supposed to tell you to rest your arm and stay off your feet, but something tells me giving advice to this group is pointless. Just try to use it as little as possible. Your cut is very deep. If you take a fever, you need to come back."

"All right. Thank you, Doctor…"

"Larson."

"Larson. Thank you."

He inclined his head to me.

I eyed my jacket. Until Grand-mère had time to give it a good stitching, it wasn't going to be of any help. I left it behind. Pulling on my cloak, I crossed the room to Agent Rose who was waiting with Edwin and Harper.

"Clemeny," Harper said, standing.

Edwin lay unconscious on the bed.

"Agent Rose told me Her Majesty asked for me."

I nodded. "She wants you here. Rose and I are going to the tower now. I'll send along some additional agents."

"All right," Harper said, barely meeting my eye.

"How is he?" I asked, glancing down at Edwin.

"Unconscious, but alive," Harper said. "Clem…"

"It's all right. I love you, and I care about him. Just watch out for the godmother. She's *awful*."

At that, Harper laughed nervously.

"We need to go," Agent Rose said.

I nodded.

"Be careful, partner," Harper told me.

"You too," I replied, then Agent Rose and I headed across the room.

"That was kind of you," Agent Rose commented.

"What else could I say? I let Edwin go. He and Harper found one another. Besides, I have someone."

"That you do. Still, it's not easy to let go of someone you once loved."

I was just about to grab for the door when it swung wide open.

On the other side was His Highness, Prince Albert.

"Agent Louvel," he said. "I heard the Red Capes were here. Are you all right?"

"Yes, Your Highness. Thank you. The others will convalesce here until we get this mess sorted."

"Yes, the Queen informed me that—" he began but stopped cold when his eyes fell on Agent Rose. "Aurora," he said in a voice barely above a whisper.

"Albert," she replied, her words lacking her usual confidence.

The two stared at one another for so long it became awkward.

I coughed lightly.

"Right," Agent Rose said. "We need to go. Good to see you, Your Highness," she said, doing an awkward little half-curtsey before she beelined past me out of the room.

"Your Highness," I said, then followed behind Rose who was walking quickly toward the door. I fell into pace with her and had just opened my mouth when Agent Rose lifted her hand.

"Not. A. Word," she told me.

"Curiouser and curiouser," I muttered with a grin.

"Oh, Agent Louvel, you have no idea."

CHAPTER 24
Tinker's Tower

The lift carried me and Agent Rose to the uppermost floor of Tinker's Tower. Even from inside the lift, I could hear the clockwork mechanisms ticking. The Rude Mechanicals had fashioned a secret meeting room just below the clockface. The emergency headquarters hadn't been used in my lifetime. But here we were.

The lift dinged, and Rose and I exited to find the Red Capes assembled in a room whose walls were lined with cogs and gears. A long meeting table stretched down the center of the room. Flickering gaslamps lit the space. Bronze-colored pipes led in every direction overhead. The furniture was dated. On the wall hung a painting of Queen Anne. But under that image was a round, bronze emblem with an R.M. encapsulated in a circle: The Rude Mechanicals. The longer I worked for the agency, the more I came to understand who they were. In a way, they were our founding fathers. Their society went back many, many years, picking up where other groups who'd sought to protect the realm had left off. The Rude Mechanicals guided and protected the monarch. But the Red Capes had become their sword and shield against the dangers in the kingdom. And right now, preventing a faerie unleashing havoc was the order of the day.

I scanned the room. Agents from every beat were there, even people I hardly ever saw like those who minded the mischievous mermaids off our coast and others who looked after angry spirits or even the undead. I spotted my closest colleagues, Hank, Cressida, and Agent Keung amongst the crowd. I nodded to Keung. He'd done well getting the word out to the agents.

Everyone came to attention when Rose and I entered.

"Everyone, please take a seat," I said, motioning to the table.

Agent Rose retreated into the shadows, leaning against a pillar not far away. Above us—or maybe it was all around us—the massive clock of Tinker's Tower ticked.

Agent Keung spoke first. "I have sent word to Shadow Watch."

I nodded to him. "Thank you."

"How is Agent Hunter? Agent Greystock?" Pippa, another agent, asked.

"Both are convalescing at Buckingham," I told them.

"Clemeny, what's going on?" one of the agents called.

"We are under attack by a rogue faerie. Prince Melwas of the Unseelie is seeking to gather the pieces of an artifact that will aid him in re-opening the gates to the Otherworld, allowing dark creatures into our world."

That silenced the room.

"What about the artifacts?" someone called.

"He recovered the first piece from our offices in India. And he got the second piece during his assault on headquarters."

"To what end?" another agent called. "What does he want?"

"I believe his goal is to destroy mankind's dominion in this realm and rule us all," I answered.

No one spoke a word.

Our job was hard, but this was beyond anything we ever expected.

"The good news is that he doesn't have the third piece," I said.

"And where is the third piece?" an agent called.

"Until an hour ago, it was hanging off Her Majesty's

neck," I said then glanced up at the portrait of Queen Anne. I had never noticed before, but she, too, was wearing the faerie gem.

"Where is it now?" Claire—Agent Monroe—asked.

I looked at Agent Rose who nodded.

I pulled the necklace out from under my shirt. "On the decoy," I said.

Everyone stared at me.

"Does it always glow like that?" Agent Fox asked.

I balked. What could I possibly say?

"It started glowing when Melwas activated the other two pieces," Agent Rose interjected.

I didn't dare look at her for fear that my expression might give away the lie. In a room full of people whose job it was to hunt the preternatural, perhaps it wasn't the best idea to start talking about faerie magic and Avalon. At least, not yet. And I knew that Agent Rose understood that very problem well.

"I managed to convince Her Majesty to give the amulet to me. We had to get it away from the Queen or Melwas would most certainly try to kill her," I said.

Agent Estcourt, who tracked demons, spoke up. "What do we do now? Who is in charge? Have the Rude Mechanicals—"

"Her Majesty promoted Clemeny to director," Agent Rose answered.

That silenced the room for a moment. I was relieved

to see the other agents nodding or smiling lightly. I met Agent Keung's eye. Grinning, he inclined his head to me.

"We're happy to have you, Clemeny—er, Agent Louvel, I mean, Director Louvel. But will Agent Hunter be all right?" Agent White asked.

I nodded. "Just Clemeny. Agent Hunter is in good hands. He was wounded, but he will recover."

"Well, Director, tell us what to do," Agent Keung said.

"Clemeny. Agent Harper is at Buckingham. Let's get some extra help out there to make sure our monarch and our own people are safe," I said, turning to Hank and Cressida. "Can you please see to that?"

They both nodded.

"The faerie has all the dark blood in the city wound up. We all need to be on guard. The Dark Districts look like the American Wild West right now."

"Yeah, I noticed," Agent Estcourt interrupted, pointing to a fresh-looking black eye.

"We know the boggarts are working with Melwas. We must get them rounded up and out of the way. Pippa, I need you and Claire to take the lead on that. Otherwise, everyone else needs to talk to their contacts and get the Dark Districts locked down. The preternatural community needs to see we have this under control. I want everyone in the streets. Be proactive."

"Director, what are you going to do?" Cressida asked.

"Clemeny. I'm going to make a very public showing of taking the stone out of the city. Whoever has eyes on us needs to see that this pendant is not around Victoria's neck anymore."

"Where will you go, Director?" Agent Keung asked.

"Clemeny. To Glastonbury."

Everyone in the room eyed me curiously.

"The druids...this is partially their mess. I'm going to make sure they help clean it up."

"You have very wide acquaintances, Director Louvel," Agent Keung said with a shake of his head. "The druids are neutral, at best. You're going to need backup."

"Did you send my messenger by airship?"

Agent Keung nodded.

"Then my backup is on its way."

"Who?" Agent Estcourt asked.

"The Pellinores."

Several agents shifted, and a few laughed uncomfortably.

"And me," Agent Rose said, nodding to me.

That brought a few whispers from the crowd.

"Then I have all the help I need," I said, nodding gratefully to her. "I will meet with the Templars and ask that they aid in getting the city under control. I am sure they will appreciate it if you give them…latitude," I said, eyeing the agents hard. I didn't care what they thought about my werewolf allies. They would respect the Templar Knights.

The group—for the most part—nodded.

"I'll be out of the city by tonight. Agent Keung, connect with Agent Harper. You will be the liaison between the Red Capes and Her Majesty while I'm off fighting faerie princes," I said, looking toward him.

He inclined his head to me, a grateful smile on his lips. Agent Keung was well-liked, skilled, and good at diplomacy. If Her Majesty hadn't noticed him already, it was time.

"This is just another case. We'll handle it. Just do your job like you always do. I have faith in all of you," I told them.

"And we have faith in you, Director," Hank called.

The other agents banged their fists on the table in support of his words.

I swallowed hard and willed my cheeks not to get red. I wished Quinn were here to see this.

"Thank you. Meeting adjourned," I said then motioned to Agent Rose. It was time to go.

The other agents stayed behind a moment, talking to one another.

Agent Keung caught up with me and Agent Rose.

"I'll head to the palace directly. Is there anything else I can do?" he asked.

"The Pellinores must meet me at the airship towers by six o'clock."

"I'll see to it."

"Thank you," I said.

With a nod, I turned to go. Agent Rose and I climbed back into the lift and began our descent back down into the city.

"That went well, *Director*," Agent Rose said, a playful smile on her lips.

"Say that again, and I'll ask you why you and Prince Albert are on a first name basis."

Agent Rose grinned.

"Well, I didn't throw up. And no one outright rejected me. So as long as Melwas doesn't take my head in order to get this little gem," I said, slipping it back inside my shirt, "I might actually get to be director."

"Let's make sure that happens."

"I need to make a couple of stops before we leave."

The lift reached the bottom. I set my hand on my pistol, waiting as the doors opened.

Nothing.

The secure location had not been compromised.

"Then I'll see you soon," Agent Rose said with a nod then headed back out onto the London street. She blended in with the crowd—which seemed impossible given her extremely striking beauty—and disappeared. I stared after her. But she was gone. That was a neat trick.

I set my hand on the amulet hidden under my shirt. When I did so, I could feel the bloody thing beating.

Today was turning out to be a very, very strange day.

Director Clemeny Louvel.

Or would it be Director Clemeny Spencer?

If I lived.

I would live. And I'd have that damned faerie's head on a pike. Firming my resolve, I turned and headed back into the city.

CHAPTER 25
Always Toward the Danger

Grand-mère was humming as she worked in the garden. The rich scents of soil filled the air. Though it was still cool, the trees in Vesta's Grotto had already bloomed with chartreuse-colored leaves and pink-and-white blossoms.

"What are you planting?" I asked as I approached.

"Oranges and lemons!" Grand-mère exclaimed, nearly tossing her trowel into the air. "You nearly scared me to death. Why are you sneaking around like that?"

"I'm not sneaking."

"Well, you didn't have to come up on me so light-footed."

"Sorry. Occupational hazard. I'll tromp next time."

Grand-mère muttered under her breath in French then paused to study me. "What's wrong?"

"Nothing...well, no. That's not true. Not nothing."

Where to start?

Grand-mère set her hand on her chest. "Oh, my Clemeny, don't tell me you've called it off with the professor now. I don't know what I'm going to do with you. I'll need to pay a visit to Quinn. You have to get sorted out—"

"No, Grand-mère. Everything is fine between myself and Professor Spencer. There was an incident at work."

"Incident?"

"A number of agents were injured...including Agent Greystock."

Grand-mère set down her tools and began pulling off her work apron. "Where is she?"

"You can't do anything right now," I said, setting my hand on her arm. "She's at Buckingham. Her Majesty's people are seeing to those who were hurt."

"And Harper? And Agent Hunter?"

"Agent Hunter was wounded as well, but he's recovering. Harper is there with the others."

Grand-mère frowned heavily. "I'm glad you're all right. Do you know what happened?"

"There was an attack on the agency headquarters. We'll be handling it."

"We? Oh, no, my girl. This sounds very dangerous. You can't go. Tell them you have a fever. Yes. That should work. Tell them you can't come because you have a fever."

"Grand-mère, I can't tell them I have a fever. I—"

"Yes, that is exactly what you'll tell them. You'll stay here in bed. You look tired anyway—"

"Grand-mère, I can't tell them I have a fever because Her Majesty promoted me to director."

At that, Grand-mère stopped. She stared at me for a long moment. Clapping the dirt off her hands one last time, she linked her arm with mine, then we headed in the direction of the house.

"I'll make you a filet. Whatever you need to do, my dear, you'll do better with a little meat in your stomach. Eliza always told me you'd replace her one day. And now…well, if Her Majesty has faith in you, I won't get in the way. But I'm not sending you out there to fight on an empty stomach."

"I hardly have time—"

"Come."

"Yes, Grand-mère," I replied with a grin.

My grandmother pinched my cheek but said nothing more.

After Grand-mère felt reassured I was adequately fed, she let me go.

"I still say it's too cold for the steamcycle," she said,

shaking her head, her hands on her hips as she watched me top off the fluids on the cycle.

"I'm not disagreeing. It's just that Harper has the auto and the agency transport is compromised."

"And where are you going, exactly?"

"Glastonbury," I replied.

"Again?"

"Yes."

"And just what's in Glastonbury that's so important?"

Druids. Gateways to the Otherworld. The mythical land of Avalon. Probably a few monsters.

"We expect our mark to be there," I said.

Because I was going to make sure he followed me there.

"Stay in the grotto until I get back. Don't wander about the city right now. It isn't safe."

"But I'm expected at Saint Clement Danes."

"Send a note. I know, tell them you have a fever."

"Clemeny."

"I'm not joking. Stay in the grotto."

Grand-mère sighed. "All right. When you see Eliza, tell her I'll come to her as soon as I can."

I nodded then kissed Grand-mère on the cheek. "Be safe," I told her.

"You too. I love you, my Clemeny."

"I love you too," I said then slipped on the cycle

Grand-mère shook her head. "You're going to freeze."

"It's only until I get to the airship."

"Airship! Don't forget the ginger."

"Never," I said with a grin then turned on the cycle. It heaved and knocked as the pipes warmed then let out a puff of steam. Pulling down my goggles, I gave Grand-mère a wave then headed across town to Temple Square.

In my rearview mirror, I watched Grand-mère close and lock the gate to the grotto.

Assured of her safety, I pulled the amulet out from under my shirt and let it dangle from my neck.

"All right, Melwas," I said to the absent prince. "Come and get me."

I PULLED THE STEAMCYCLE INTO TEMPLE SQUARE. THE place was busy. As soon as one of the wolves spotted me, he rushed into the hall. Lionheart exited immediately thereafter.

"Clemeny," he said as he moved to meet me. "We just heard."

I nodded. "Red Cape headquarters was attacked," I said. "Several agents were injured. Melwas was after something."

"Did he get it?"

"Unfortunately."

Lionheart eyed the pendant. "That's new." He reached out to touch it but pulled his hand back. "What is that?" he asked, a low growl in his voice.

"A faerie gem. And the last piece of the device Melwas needs."

"Why is it hanging around your neck?"

"Because I'm about to take an airship back to Glastonbury. I'm hoping Melwas will follow."

Lionheart frowned. "I understand that Conklin was in on the attack."

I nodded. "Unfortunately. Acwellen and two of his pack brothers are dead."

Lionheart frowned. "The city is upside down. The packs and every other damned thing are stirred up."

I nodded. "The Red Capes are coming. I asked them to give the Templars leeway."

"Very good. I'll inform Blackwood then get my things."

"I thought…you're needed here."

"Victoria put a noose around your neck. There is no way I'm letting you out of my sight."

"Richard," I said, taking his hand. "I'll be all right. Agent Rose, Constantine, and the Pellinores will come with me to—"

Lionheart set his hand on my cheek. "I know you'll be all right, but Clemeny…"

I knew him well enough to know he still blamed himself for what happened to Bryony. But I wasn't Bryony. And there was someone else to consider.

"I must go. I have to get this out of the city. Richard, I know you want to be with me, but Jericho… We can't leave him alone, not with so much danger everywhere."

Lionheart inhaled slowly as he thought over my words. After a moment, he nodded. "I will come with you to the airship towers."

"I need to be there soon."

Lionheart pulled out his pocket watch. "I'll talk to Blackwood now."

"Where is Jericho?" I asked.

"In the garden pretending to study," Lionheart replied, pointing over his shoulder. I turned toward the garden while Lionheart headed to Middle Hall. I could hear the sound of a ball bouncing even before I arrived. The book and notepaper lay forgotten on a bench not far away. Picking up the forgotten tome, I read the title aloud, "*The Adventures of King Arthur and His Knights.*"

Jericho jumped, startled by the sound of my voice, then turned and looked at me. To my surprise, I saw the glimmer of red in his eyes.

"Clemeny. You startled me."

"Sorry about that. How's the book?"

Jericho snorted.

I chuckled. "I was never the scholarly type either. But *The Adventures of King Arthur and His Knights* sounds like a good one."

"I liked the story about the sword."

"Excalibur?"

Jericho nodded. "King Arthur was just an orphan. Everyone was always mean to him. And then one day, the Lady of the Lake gave Excalibur to Arthur, and he used it to protect the whole country."

I looked down at the tattered text, a swell of mixed emotions rising up in me. "It's a nice fairy tale."

"Fairy tale? Sir Richard told me it was a history lesson."

"I suppose that depends on whether or not you believe King Arthur was a real king, or if he's just a fable."

"Of course he was a real king," Jericho told me, his voice filled with exasperation. "What is it that you're wearing?"

"Speaking of fairy tales." I lay the pendant in my hand. "Listen. Can you hear it?"

"What is that?"

"It's a faerie gem."

"Something about that stone isn't right."

I nodded. "You're correct. I need to take the stone out of the city, get it away from everyone."

"So…so, you're leaving the city?"

"Just for a little while."

"Is Sir Richard going with you?"

"No. He's going to go with me to the airship towers, but he'll be back."

"I want to come."

I shook my head. "Not this time, my dear."

"But Clemeny…"

"I promised Afwyn I would keep you safe. Keeping you safe means leaving you here under the care of the Templars. When I get back, when all of this is done, then maybe things will be different."

"You'll come here and stay with us?"

That was never going to happen.

"I don't know, but I do know I want to be closer to you and Sir Richard. I miss you when we're not together."

"I miss you too," he said then wrapped his arms around my waist. "Wherever you're going, please be careful."

"I will."

"Clemeny…please come back," he whispered, his voice cracking a little.

A knot rose in my throat, and I swallowed hard. "Of course," I said then kissed him on the top of his head.

A moment later, we heard footsteps approach. I

kissed the boy once more then let him go. Lionheart entered the garden.

"Jericho, Sir Blackwood would like you to join the other Templars at Middle Hall. They're holding a meeting."

"About what?" Jericho asked.

"Some wolves in the city are misbehaving. He is assigning tasks to the pack. Sir Blackwood needs all the Templars here."

"Including me?" Jericho asked, his eyes wide.

"Yes, including you."

The boy moved as if he wanted to bolt to the meeting hall, but then he paused and looked at Lionheart. "You'll be back, right?"

Lionheart nodded. "I'll return very soon. You'll be safe with the brotherhood."

Jericho rushed to Lionheart, giving him a quick hug. "Please be careful," he said then raced toward the hall.

"Is Briarwood really going to put him to work?" I asked, feeling concerned.

Lionheart nodded. "Yes, as a lookout, safely inside Temple Square."

"Ahh," I said then nodded.

"You were followed here," Lionheart said as we headed back to the gate. "A boggart is lingering just outside. I told the others to leave him be."

"Did he really think that a pack of werewolves wouldn't notice him?"

"Apparently. Shapeshifters are good at what they do—shifting form—but aren't very bright. They forget what good noses we have."

We headed back to the steamcycle.

"After you," Lionheart said, motioning for me to drive.

I raised an eyebrow at him.

I mounted the cycle then adjusted the mirrors. The pack was right. There was a gentleman at a shoeshine stand down the street who was not getting his shoes polished. He was just sitting. Watching.

Lionheart wrapped his arms around me then sighed happily.

"Now I know why you let me drive," he said, firmly holding my waist.

"Oh, Sir Richard, you haven't seen anything yet."

CHAPTER 26
All Aboard

Lionheart and I arrived at the central London airship towers just before six o'clock. Overhead, airships of all sizes, from single-person crafts to massive international ships, floated in and out of the port. The scarlet balloon of the agency airship was clearly noticeable on the platform reserved for official government or emergency business. I parked the steamcycle then grabbed my gear.

As Lionheart and I headed toward the lift, I scanned the crowd.

"We're not alone," Lionheart said.

He was right. I felt it too. The airship towers were a hotbed for preternatural miscreants, many of whom likely had nothing to do with Melwas and his plans to swarm the known world with all sorts of maleficent creatures.

I eyed the crowd as we made our way toward the lift. A moment later, Agent Rose fell into step with us.

"Louvel," she said then eyed Lionheart. "And Alpha," she added, inclining her head to Lionheart who returned the gesture.

"Any guesses on what's creeping around?" I asked her.

"Besides the three of us?" she replied with a light laugh. "Well, the Pellinores have some interesting guests. At least three boggarts are watching them. I spotted a banshee, but I think she's hovering about some airship pirates pretending to be traders. There are two goblin pickpockets working the crowd. The American trading vessel seems to have brought along some sort of shapeshifter I've never seen the likes of before, but he's pretending to be a human and definitely didn't want me to notice him. And a partridge in a pear tree."

Lionheart chuckled lightly.

Given my history with the *Twelve Days of Christmas,* I was less amused.

"Oh, and the boggart who arrived just behind you," Agent Rose added.

"And Melwas?"

Agent Rose shook her head. "Not here. He was spotted in the Dark District after the attack on the agency but not since."

I frowned. "Let's go up," I said, pointing to the lift.

The lift operator, spying my and Agent Rose's red capes, opened the lift gate but said nothing. Not making eye contact with any of us, he took us up to the platform where our colleagues waited.

On the platform just outside the agency airship, I spotted Agent Keung.

And Harper.

They walked down the platform toward us.

"Harper, what are you doing here?" I asked.

"Once I heard the plan, I asked Her Majesty's permission to come join you. I can't have my partner out risking her neck while I'm sitting around drinking tea."

"And keeping our colleagues safe," I said.

"I agreed to take over Harper's duties," Agent Keung told me.

"And agents from Shadow Watch have arrived," Harper added. "Shadow Watch is cleaning up the tunnels and securing headquarters. Except Agent Walsh's unit. I sent him to the sewers."

"But we didn't have any issues in the sewers," Agent Keung said.

Harper grinned. "No. We did not."

I laughed. Served Agent Walsh right for making Harper and me take the *back entrance* into Shadow Watch Headquarters.

"Shadow Watch also has agents at Buckingham," she said then turned to Lionheart. "I directed them to be cooperative with the Templars."

Lionheart nodded.

"Thank you. I'm glad you're here," I told Harper. In a way, I was happy something blossomed between her and Edwin. I cared about them both, and I wanted them both to be happy. Happy together was a good thing. And if Edwin's godmother got nasty with Harper, this time there was nothing preventing me from speaking my mind. Loudly. With a pointy item in my hand.

The head of the Pellinore division, Agent Ewan Goodwin, lifted his hand in welcome. Along with Ewan, I spotted Pellinore agents Lucy Silver and William Williamson. But I wasn't looking for any of them. It was Rapunzel Pendragon, a young woman with a massive mop of golden hair—and her faerie companion—for whom I was searching. Both were on the airship.

"Agent Louvel," Agent Goodwin called, moving toward me. His eyes turned from me to Lionheart. I saw him take in the werewolf and debate what to do. In the end, he gave Lionheart a polite nod.

Lionheart huffed lightly under his breath.

"Agents," I said, nodding to Agents Goodwin, Silver, and Williamson. "Thank you for coming."

"I understand we're headed to Glastonbury," Agent Goodwin said.

"Indeed we are," I answered, my eyes flicking toward Miss Pendragon once more.

Agent Goodwin nodded nervously then rubbed the back of his neck. "Agent Keung updated us on what happened at the agency. We're ready to help. All of us," he said, looking back at the pair on the airship.

"I'm counting on it," I said.

"Something tells me we're in for a fight, Agent Louvel," Agent Williamson said.

"Wherever would you get that idea?"

"Oh, just a hunch," he said, glancing from Rose to Lionheart. He shrugged. "Pellinores owe you one for that mess at Willowbrook anyway. Better come aboard and tell us what's going on."

I looked from Rose to Harper. "Shall we?" I asked, motioning to the airship.

Harper nodded then boarded the ship.

"I'm headed back to Buckingham," Agent Keung told me.

"I'll come with you," Agent Rose told him.

"You're not coming?" I asked Rose.

"I'll be there. Later. With my backup," she said, motioning to the sky overhead. "We're nightshift."

Ahh.

"See you later, Louvel," Agent Rose said, then she and Agent Keung left.

"Just a moment," I said then turned to Lionheart.

We stepped away from the others for a moment.

"You know, I remember you standing on the roof of that hangar," Lionheart said, motioning to the yard behind us where the Templars and I had fought the wizard Marlowe. "It's quite possible that was the moment I fell in love with you."

"At that moment? Why?"

"Because I came to do battle with a wizard and all the werewolves in London. And so had you. The only difference was that I came with an army. You were all alone, your red cape swirling around you. You looked like David about to take on Goliath. And there was not a flicker of fear in your eyes. I don't think I've admired anyone more in my entire life."

"Well, considering how long your life has been, that's saying something."

"Those age jokes will never grow tired," he said with a light laugh.

"I certainly hope not. How about now? Any flickering in my eyes?" I asked, gazing up at him.

"Very certainly, but those sparks have nothing to do with fear."

I winked at Lionheart. "Then let's get this over with. We have the rest of our lives waiting for us."

He smiled softly at me. "Be careful."

"Of course."

"I love you."

"I love you too," I whispered in reply then turned and headed toward the airship.

CHAPTER 27
At Least It's Not Lord Cabell

I boarded the airship, motioning to the captain that we were ready for departure. Steadying myself at the rail, I dipped into my pocket for a ginger chew. The burner under the balloon fired, and the airship lifted out of port, heaving us up into the sky as the vessel turned west, my stomach turning along with it. Holding onto the ropes, I gazed out at the city. It would be dark soon. Arriving at Glastonbury at night was not ideal. And I had no idea what the druids were going to think about me bringing the fight to them. But everything in me told me I needed to get Melwas away from the city, away from the agency, away from my Queen, away from my so—Jericho, and somewhere… thin. Somewhere where the veil between the worlds could be easily opened and closed. Somewhere like Glastonbury.

Harper came and stood beside me.

"If I never have to board an airship again, it will be too soon," I grumbled.

"Well, at least this time we aren't hunting Vikings."

"Luring someone who wants to unleash the apocalypse to follow us is better?"

"Not when you put it that way. What if he doesn't follow us?"

I looked down at the crowd moving busily at the base of the airship towers. I could feel the preternaturals there. And while I couldn't actually see Melwas, I knew. He was watching.

"He'll be there."

"Should I tell the captain to watch for someone following us?"

I shook my head. "No. No fussing about on an airship for him. He has his device."

"He could get the drop on us, be there before we get there," Harper said, worry in her voice.

"He might. And he won't even have to get airsick in the process."

Harper sighed. She was silent for a long time before she said, "Clemeny, do you want to talk—"

I shook my head. "There is nothing to talk about. I just wish you'd told me sooner."

"That's what Edwin said."

"He was right. I'm not upset. I'm glad, actually."

"Well, you won't be completely glad."

"And why not?"

"Because I'm going to go to India with Edwin."

"Don't they have mummies there?"

"That's Egypt, not India. We want a clean break… that's part of the reason Edwin asked for the transfer."

"I see."

"Are…are you angry?"

"Yes, that I'm losing my partner."

"But you're director now. You won't need a partner. And Agent Rose always seems to have an eye out for you."

"So she does."

"I'm sorry things got…messy."

"No. I'm glad it worked out like this. I was worried you were secretly dating Lord Cabell."

"Oh, good god. No."

At that, we both laughed.

"Messy, I understand. Believe me. I'm happy for you, Elaine. And for Edwin."

"Thank you," she said with a relieved sigh.

A soft hand touched my arm.

I turned to find Gothel standing there. She was a tall woman with dark hair, a lithe frame, and glimmering eyes that had a sheen of quicksilver. I had met her the summer before when some werewolves had abducted her for a bit of coin. That had not ended well for them.

Gothel, as it turned out, was the protector of the line of Pendragon and had been roaming about the realm since the sixth century. The current heir of Pendragon, the sweet young girl with the longest yellow hair I had ever seen, was sitting on the other side of the airship smiling lovingly at Agent Goodwin. Good lord, were all Red Cape agents destined to fall in love with the very preternaturals we hunted?

"Clemeny," Gothel said, looking at the amulet, her eyes wide. "What you are wearing is very dangerous."

"Is it going to explode or anything?" I asked.

The faerie paused, surprised by my question. "No, but—"

"I know. Melwas will take my head for it. That's why it's around my neck and not Victoria's."

"I see," Gothel said, sighing lightly.

"What do you know about Melwas?" I asked the faerie.

"He has always been the outcast of the Unseelie Court. Unruly, angry. He despises mankind. Queen Macha, his mother, has failed to rule or turn him. He is loved by the dark things of the Unseelies and the dark things of this realm. Even the blood of Mordred—the dragon bloods—honored him. They were his allies until they were defeated," she said, glancing over her shoulder at the three Pellinore agents and Miss Pendragon who had seen to the exile of the dragon bloods. "If he has the other two pieces of the artifact, he will stop at nothing to take the gem from you. Including killing you and any of us who get in his way."

"Aren't you glad I asked you to come?" I replied.

Gothel smiled lightly. "I know why you asked us to come. I know what the druids have told you."

"And?"

Gothel tapped her fingers on the rail of the airship. "Once, long ago, Melwas tried to abduct Gwenhwyfar, the white phantom. She was the wife of King Arthur. I was her protector. I didn't let him win then, and I won't let him win now. And I never had the chance to properly thank him for trying to kidnap my charge."

I raised an eyebrow at the faerie.

"We all have our reasons for being here," she said, a light smile on her face.

"Well, then. I guess we shall see."

Gothel nodded. "We shall see."

CHAPTER 28
Glastonbury Tor

It was already dark when the agency airship swooped in low over Abbey House. The night's sky was filled with stars, but there was a distant rumble on the horizon. From the east, a storm was blowing in. I could see the dark clouds gathering, rolling as they moved west. Lightning rocked the clouds, which twisted and turned unnaturally.

There was no tower at which to port, so the airship captain threw a rope ladder over the side.

"I'll do my best to hold her steady, Agents," he called to us. "But there's a storm coming in. You need to be quick about it. There's a port in town. I'll take the airship there."

"Thank you," Harper called to the captain then nodded to us.

One by one, we hurried down the ladder to the ground.

When I reached the Tor, I turned and watched the oncoming storm. The wind whipped hard, blowing my cape all around me.

"It's Melwas," Gothel said.

I nodded.

"Well, you're right about him following the gem," Harper said as she eyed the oncoming storm.

"You see, having a decoy works. It worked at the museum opening," I said.

"I thought you said that was a terrible plan," Harper retorted.

"It was, because Victoria was the bait that time. The plan was good. The bait was the problem."

Harper shook her head. "Okay, bait. What now?"

"Into the ruins," I said, motioning for the others to follow me.

The burner under the airship hissed then the ship set off in the direction of the town. I looked behind me at Abbey House. In an upstairs window of the house, I spotted the silhouette of Mister Reeves.

I waved to him.

He lifted his hand to return the gesture.

As we moved deeper into the ruins, a terrible feeling swept over me.

Mist began to snake around the rubble as the sky overhead became overcast. The clouds gathered, blocking out the stars. Thunder rumbled. The clouds twisted unnaturally. My scalp, palms, and bottoms of my feet felt prickly.

Agents Williamson and Silver drew their weapons.

Melwas knew where I was going. There was already something here, something amongst the ruins.

Rapunzel and Gothel joined Harper and me.

Rapunzel stared out at the ruins. "What is this place?" she whispered.

"These are the ruins of Glastonbury Abbey. But on the Otherside is the Isle of Glass. That is what my people call it. Your people call it Avalon," Gothel told her.

"Avalon," Rapunzel said, her voice full of awe. She turned to me. "I think…I think I know why you asked me to come."

I smiled at her. "Good. Because I'm just playing a hunch."

Thunder overhead rumbled as the massive clouds extinguished the moonlight that had been casting a little glow. The fog snaked around us, moving unnaturally. There was a sick, pungent scent in the air.

"Not good," Agent Goodwin said, pulling on his own pair of night-vision goggles. Seemed I wasn't the only one getting the good tech these days.

From somewhere deep within the mist, I heard a low growl.

"Really not good," Agent Goodwin repeated.

I scanned the ruins. The mist moved, shifting as if something had passed through it.

A moment later, I heard a strange, strangled growl and something with glimmering eyes bounded toward Agent Silver.

"Lucy, watch out," Agent Goodwin called, lifting his pistol.

The manticore leaped toward the agent. Goodwin's aim was true. The beast fell. But it soon became clear we were not alone. Low growls and flashing eyes surrounded us. There were beasts everywhere.

"Hell's bells," I whispered.

"We're ambushed," Agent Williamson said.

"Maybe," I answered then pulled the faerie dagger from my belt. The metal glowed blue. "But it's not over yet," I said then turned and rushed the closest beast.

THE FIREFIGHT THAT ENSUED THEREAFTER WAS PRACTICALLY a blur. Harper, Goodwin, Williamson, and Silver followed my lead and advanced on the monsters. Out of the corner of my eye, I saw Gothel summon her magic. A glimmer of blue light sparked between her fingers.

With Rapunzel—who held a sword before her—close by, the faerie joined the fight.

This time, it wasn't just manticores. Four-legged creatures with slick ebony skin, defying any description I had ever heard or read about, attacked. Scaled monsters that seemed to be made up entirely of claws and teeth joined the assault. The monsters were from the Otherworld. Strange, fey things that didn't exist even in our mythology. This is what the mortal realm would face if Melwas succeeded. We couldn't let that happen. I turned to find a winged manticore like I had encountered in the tunnel creeping slowly up on me. Catlike, it moved to pounce.

I spun out of the way, ducking into the ruins of Glastonbury Abbey. I raced through the narrow corridor of one of the abbey's partially fallen structures, and the monster charged after me. It smashed the ruin with its body, further collapsing the structure.

"Dammit, this is an important historical monument," I called to the monster in frustration, turning to face the beast before it did any more damage.

The monster burst out of the narrow corridor then slid to a stop. It let out a strange clicking call, then a moment later, two other dark shadows appeared, their eyes glowing.

"Hell's bells," I whispered, backing up. "Umm, Harper?" I called.

"Clemeny? Clemeny, where are you?"

"A little help?"

"Clemeny? Where are you? I can't see anything."

Brandishing my dagger, I stepped back.

Time to run.

Realizing his prey was going to try to escape, the largest of the manticores pounced.

I turned and ran. Slipping over ruins and between stone arches, I hurried away. But the beasts were catching up, and I was running out of ruins to hide behind. On top of that, it was bloody dark and foggy. I could hardly see where I was going.

I spun and stopped, looking over my shoulder just in time to see one of the winged manticores launch at me.

I was too late.

The one time I had run from the danger, I was going to die.

"Richard," I whispered, closing my eyes.

A cool breeze swept over me. And with it, I heard the sound of a thousand tiny wings and the shrieking of bats.

Gasping, I opened my eyes once more.

Agent Rose was standing in front of me, a grin on her face. "Stop standing around," she said then turned and attacked one of the beasts.

The colony of bats swarmed the winged beast who

had leaped at me. Within, I spotted the vampire, Constantine.

I moved toward the third beast who looked confused and dismayed by the sudden appearance of my allies. Taking advantage of his momentary confusion, I attacked. Jumping up on one of the ruins, I raced down the length of the stone then leaped onto the monster's back, slicing the sharp point off his vicious tail before he had a chance to strike. The creature howled. I put an end to his wretched noise by stabbing him through the back of the neck.

"We have to help Harper and the others," I called to Rose and Constantine then rushed toward the sound of the firefight underway.

As we raced to join the others, I couldn't help but notice the waver in the air. The boundaries between this world and the other world were growing thinner. In brief glimpses, I caught sight of the standing stones in Avalon. But I also saw something more. Between such glimpses, I saw a darker place. I couldn't see it well, but I could smell the heavy scent of earth and rot that always effervesced from that world, the land of the Unseelie.

I rushed back to find Harper and Agent Silver barely holding their own against some sort of double-headed canine. Agent Goodwin was facing down his own manticore. Agent Williamson, Gothel, and Rapunzel were surrounded.

I stared as the faerie shot blasts of blue light from her hands.

But it was Rapunzel who drew my attention. The girl's long locks were glowing.

And she was…singing.

Agent Rose, Constantine, and I all stopped and stared.

"Is she singi—" Agent Rose began, but a strange sound cut her words short.

A massive roar, which I felt from deep within me, made the very land around me quiver.

"What was that?" Constantine whispered.

A moment later, a massive fireball blasted from the dark sky. And then another. And another.

Rapunzel lifted off the ground, and a moment later, four dragons, each as big as a carriage, swarmed around her. She shouted to them, and the dragons attacked the Unseelie beasts.

"Mother of God," Agent Rose exclaimed. "You didn't tell us about the dragons."

"I didn't have a chance…and they were kitten-sized the last time I saw them."

Lightning cracked overhead, and the ground shook.

All of us pitched sideways, and suddenly my head became a blurry mess. I tried to right myself, but everything was fuzzy. I saw the ruins of Glastonbury Abbey and the standing stones of Avalon all at once.

"Clemeny," Harper called, moving toward me.

A sick feeling rocked my stomach.

The world around me shuddered once more, and the ruins of Glastonbury Abbey began to fade away.

Clemeny. Clemeny Louvel.

He's here.

The ground below my feet trembled.

And then, everything grew silent.

I was standing in Avalon amongst the monoliths.

And standing just across from me was Melwas.

CHAPTER 29
Melwas

I inhaled slowly, trying to center myself. My head was swimming, and I was still half-nauseous from the airship ride. Suddenly being yanked into Avalon wasn't helping. I stilled, letting my senses come into focus. The sky here was clear, a blanket of stars twinkling overhead. The full moon shone down brightly upon me.

The sounds of the battle rolled like a distant echo across the horizon. The others were so very far from me.

"Thank you for bringing me the gemstone, Agent Louvel," Melwas said.

His eyes glimmered bluish-silver in the moonlight, the strange runes on his skin taking on a similar glow.

The wind blew softly. His white hair whipped around him.

I exhaled slowly then smiled. "You're rather

confused, Melwas. I believe you're here to give the artifact back to me."

The faerie smirked then pulled out the device from his robe. "Right here," he said, tapping the device. "That's where the stone will go. I don't think it will mind a little blood on it, if that's what it takes."

"We'll see," I said then held the faerie dagger before me.

"Going to try to kill me with my own dagger? That's a nice touch."

"I do my best with irony," I said, and without waiting another moment, I attacked.

I knew from my first encounter with the faerie that he was strong and fast. He ducked and swept to the side, but I had expected the move. Kicking out my leg, I caught the faerie unexpectedly, tripping him. The faerie quickly regained his footing then came at me, pulling a flashing curved knife when he did so. I pulled my pistol and took aim. The move surprised the faerie who quickly slipped behind a standing stone. I held my pistol in front of me and waited.

He didn't come out.

It was only when I smelled that terrible earthy scent that I realized what he'd done. He'd slipped between the stones and out of this world, only to reappear behind me—hell's bells.

I ducked and turned, only to feel the dagger connect with the length of my hair, slicing off my tresses.

"Oh now, that's just rude," I called.

"You're the one who brought a pistol to a knife fight," the faerie said then launched at me again.

Once more, we exchanged blows. While the faerie was quick, he hadn't spent the last several years fighting werewolves. He was fast, but I was stronger. I punched the faerie between the eyes, hard. He staggered backward then stepped between the stones, disappearing once more.

"Dammit," I said then spun all around me, waiting for him to reappear.

I was about to turn again when I felt him draw close to me.

Very close.

Hell's bells.

Something hard hit me on the back of my head.

I groaned then turned. The faerie dropped the massive rock he'd been holding then attacked, punching me in the face. I staggered backward. The blow made my jaw ache, and the salty tang of blood filled my mouth. He advanced on me again, this time with his blade in his hand. My ears rang, and the blow to my head made my vision blur. If I fainted, he would kill me and take the amulet. If I fainted, he would call forth the dark creatures and kill my friends, my family. I couldn't let that happen. I staggered, but held on, deflecting a blow that had been intended for my heart, only to feel the slick slice of a blade cut my brow. At once, blood clouded the vision of my good eye.

"Clemeny! Clemeny?" I could hear Harper calling from very far away.

"There," I heard Gothel answer. "Clemeny!"

I staggered backward, holding the faerie dagger in front of me.

"It's too late," Melwas said as he stalked toward me. "Even the faerie guardian can't stop me now. Give me the gemstone."

I backed up. Tripping over a stone, I fell to the ground, landing with a splash into a mud puddle.

"You fought well, Clemeny Louvel. But it's done. Give me the stone."

"No," I whispered.

This couldn't be happening.

It wasn't supposed to end like this.

I brought him here because I knew I could defeat him. This wasn't happening. I wasn't supposed to be covered in blood, lying in a mud puddle.

I gasped.

Looking past the faerie who was advancing menacingly, I saw the standing stones, and then I saw back to Glastonbury Abbey.

Gothel worked her hands, casting shimmering blue

light. And a moment later, Rapunzel stepped into Avalon.

Seeing what was happening, she paused.

Melwas must have sensed the presence of another because he turned and looked behind him.

"Who are you?" he asked.

For the love of all things holy, if it's true, come to me now.

Through my blood-clouded eyes, I looked down at the mud puddle in which I was sitting.

The water shivered, then I saw a glint of silver.

I plunged my hand into the water.

Suppressing my shock when my hand connected with metal, I wrapped my fingers around the pommel then rose.

The earth shuddered. The air rung with a slicing sound as I drew the sword from the belly of the earth.

I rose, Excalibur in my hand.

"Rapunzel," I called.

The girl turned to me, her eyes wide.

I threw the sword to her.

The glowing golden light from the sword reflected on Melwas's face for a brief moment.

"No," he said, turning in panic to snatch the amulet from me.

I raised my hands, and the water below my feet lifted me away from his grasp.

"Lady of the Lake," he whispered, a confused expression on his face.

The unexpected show of power knocked the faerie off guard just long enough for the heir of Pendragon to swing Excalibur.

The air shook as the sword, which had slumbered so long, awoke to strike.

Light flashed as the blade slid through the neck of the faerie prince.

He stood perfectly still for a moment, then dropped, his head tumbling to the ground.

The torrent of water that had been holding me aloft lowered me once more.

Breathing hard, Rapunzel stood there, the Sword of Kings in her hand. She stared at the decapitated body.

"What did I just do?" she whispered.

"You saved your country."

Rapunzel looked from the sword to me. "How did you...where did you get this?"

"She is the Lady of the Lake," a voice called from behind us.

Rapunzel and I both turned to see the druids I had met upon my last visit standing there. It was my aunt Nyneve who'd spoken.

Nyneve smiled at me. "I told you."

I looked at Rapunzel.

"Agent Louvel...what do I do? I don't want to be

Queen. Victoria is Queen. I don't want to be Queen," Rapunzel said.

"The sword is yours, Rapunzel Pendragon," Nyneve told her.

Rapunzel shook her head then crossed the space between us and handed Excalibur to me. "Put it back."

I hesitated. I was loyal to Her Majesty, of that there was no doubt, but Excalibur…this was something else.

"If we need it again, we'll get it again," Rapunzel said. "Please."

I stared at her for a long moment. I had not spent much time with Rapunzel when we'd last met, but there was an honesty to her nature. I looked into her eyes. The colors therein moved and turned. I had never seen anything like it. But her gaze also spoke. Just like me, she wanted to keep Britannia safe. To do so, she couldn't disrupt the monarchy. There was already a steady hand on the throne. We could protect our realm, but not by deposing our monarch and causing chaos.

Taking Excalibur, I walked over the pool of water from which I'd drawn the sword for the heir of the Once and Future King.

"No offense," I whispered to the sword. "I suspect we'll meet again," I said then dipped my hand back into the water. Somehow, that shallow pool felt bottomless. I let go of the sword, which sank back into the deep earth.

Rising once more, I wiped the blood from my eye. I

swooned a little when I stood. There was a throbbing pain blasting through my head, and my ears were ringing.

"Clemeny, you're hurt. You should come with us," Nyneve said, extending her hand to me.

I looked from her to Rapunzel then through the stones. On the other side, I could see Harper and Agent Rose looking for me.

"Clemeny? Clem, where are you?" Harper called, a look of panic on her face.

"No. But thank you," I told her then turned to Rapunzel. "Let's go."

Rapunzel nodded at me.

"Clemeny," Nyneve called gently. "You are welcome here. Please come back…when you're ready."

I inclined my head to her then bent to take the pieces of the device from Melwas' unmoving hand. When I did so, a sense of dread washed over me. Rapunzel and I had just murdered a faerie prince. Would there be a reckoning or would the Unseelie accept that Melwas had taken a risk and lost? I wasn't sure. I slipped the device into my pocket then took Rapunzel's hand.

I looked back over my shoulder at Nyneve one last time.

Maybe.

Some day.

But not today.

I nodded to Rapunzel, and together, we crossed back into the real world.

CHAPTER 30
The End is the Beginning

The moment we stepped into the ruins of Glastonbury Abbey, black spots appeared before my eyes.

"Clemeny," Harper called, rushing to me.

Agent Rose exhaled with relief, but then I saw her eyes narrow as she studied me.

I handed the pieces of the artifact to Harper. "Here. Melwas bashed me on the head with a rock, I think…" I said, unable to form words as the throbbing intensified. My vision grew dim as the black dots danced.

"Harper," Agent Rose said then moved toward me.

The world around me began to spin. "I think I'm going to—"

But before I could say the word *faint*, everything went black.

RM

I could hear Harper humming even before I opened my eyes. I was lying somewhere warm and soft. Despite this fact, my head ached terribly.

Groaning, I opened my eyes to be greeted by the soft morning light. I moved to sit up.

"Take it easy," Harper said, setting aside the pile of papers she was working on. She moved to my bedside. "Don't try to get up."

"Hell's bells," I muttered, reaching to touch the back of my head.

Harper chuckled softly. "There is a very nasty lump back there."

"Melwas," I muttered.

"Well, according to Rapunzel, you cut off his head. So I guess the two of you are even."

"Wait, Rapunzel said *I* cut off his head?"

"Um, yeah. That's what she said. Wait, are you saying—"

"Where am I?" I asked.

"Abbey House," a familiar, masculine voice called from the doorway.

Lionheart.

"Hey," I said softly.

He smiled at me. "Welcome back."

Harper looked from Lionheart to me and back again. She smiled. "All right. Well, I need to finish this paperwork anyway. I'll be downstairs if you need me."

"Harper, where is Rapunzel?" I asked.

"Gone. She left with the Pellinores. An agency airship took them back to Willowbrook Park. They said you should come visit when you feel better."

"And Agent Rose?"

"Gone too. Before dawn. Her friend with her."

I nodded.

Harper gave me a little wave, gathered up her things, then slipped out the door.

Lionheart crossed the room and sat down on my bedside. He took my hand.

"When did you get here?" I asked.

"Yesterday."

"Yesterday? How long have I been out?"

"Two days. Harper sent a messenger to London to let me know you'd been injured. Apparently, Mister Reeves took everyone in after whatever mess occurred in the ruins ended."

"What about the packs?"

"The Templars have reminded everyone that we are still in charge. The Red Capes are busy cleaning up the Dark Districts; Shadow Watch is helping. Everything is settled. Except for the fact that you've been unconscious and are sporting a fresh batch of stitches," he said, pointing to my face.

So distracted by the ache in my head, I hadn't even noticed the smarting pain just above my good eye.

"Wonderful. At least I'll be symmetrical. But I'm alive. And I got the artifact back. Harper has it."

"Except that," Lionheart said, pointing to my neck. I looked down to see I was still wearing the faerie gemstone.

"Ahh. Yes. That requires a conversation with Her Majesty."

"Which can wait until you're recovered, no matter if you're the new director of the Red Capes or not. Mister Reeves said you can stay here and rest as long as you like."

"That's very kind of him—wait, how do you know I'm the new director?"

"Grand-mère told me."

"Grand-mère?"

Lionheart chuckled. "You don't think I'd let her sit at home worrying about you. I brought her with me."

"You brought Grand-mère here?"

"Yes."

"As in, you drove her all the way out here?"

"So I did."

I laughed, but the sound of my own voice made me

wince, my head banging. "Oh, Richard. I don't know what to say."

"No matter. I have been given some specific advice on what I should be saying and doing. I say, Clemeny, if the Red Capes are in need of an interrogator, you need look no further than your grandmother. I felt almost undone when she was finished with me."

I laughed. "And what did Grand-mère decide you should be saying and doing?"

Lionheart smirked. "That is between Grand-mère and me."

The door to the bedroom banged wide open. The noise was so loud that I suppressed a shudder.

"Clemeny!" Jericho yelled, rushing to me. Pushing Lionheart aside, the boy wrapped his arms around me. "Agent Harper said you were awake."

"Easy, Jericho. Clemeny is still in pain."

"It's all right," I said, hugging the boy to me. The feel of his little body in my arms filled me with a sense of peace. I sighed.

Jericho let me go. "They said you passed out. That's a terrible cut on your eye. Did a werewolf do that?"

I shook my head. "A faerie."

Jericho scrunched up his face as he thought it over. "Where is this faerie?" he asked then, his voice sounding decidedly dark and wolf-like.

"Dealt with," I replied. "So you don't need to worry." I turned to Richard. "And just wait until I tell you how."

Richard raised an eyebrow at me.

"Oh my Clemeny, my Clemeny. Oranges and lemons, every time you go off to work, I worry I'll find you like this. And here you are all battered and bruised again," Grand-mère began before she even entered the room. Her face was a mix of sincere worry and annoyance. But she stopped in the doorway.

"Grand-mère," I said softly, smiling at her.

Grand-mère looked from Richard, to Jericho, to me. The expression on her face softened, and she smiled serenely.

"Well, my girl," she said. I was surprised to see her eyes looking watery.

"Grand-mère?"

She smiled then wiped a stray tear from her eye. "I'll ring for tea," she said then turned and headed back down the hallway.

Jericho kissed me on the cheek then jumped up. "May I ask Grand-mère to bring biscuits too?"

I nodded. "Go tell her."

Jericho placed one more quick kiss on my cheek then ran off behind Grand-mère.

Richard took his place on my bedside once more. He

stared at me for a long time then pulled me into a deep embrace.

"I love you," he whispered in my ear.

"I love you too."

Despite all the odds, I had fallen madly, deeply in love with the big bad wolf.

And he was everything to me.

TWO DAYS LATER, ONCE I WAS BACK ON MY FEET, I MET Mister Reeves to say goodbye once more. Grand-mère was chatting with Jericho as the pair climbed into the back seat of the steamauto. I hadn't heard what the boy had said, but Grand-mère laughed loudly, the sound of her happy voice echoing across the gardens.

"I hope we meet again very soon," Mister Reeves told me, reaching out to shake my hand. "But under better circumstances next time."

I nodded. "Thank you for your hospitality once more."

"Of course."

"The bags are settled. I gave the rest to Agent Harper to take with her on the airship. Otherwise, I believe we're ready," Lionheart told me.

I inclined my head to Mister Reeves then turned to

get into the steamauto. I paused one last time to look out at the ruins. It was early morning. The sunrise cast shades of pink and gold on the ruins of Glastonbury Abbey. The vision was lovely, but the longer I looked, the more the image began to waver. Once more, I spotted the standing stones in Avalon, a place of legend.

Clemeny.

Clemeny Louvel.

I shook my head. "Not today," I answered the voice on the wind. "Not yet." *Maybe never.* I turned my gaze away from the stones and back to this world. Opening the door of the auto, I smiled at the little lycan sitting in the back seat. "Have everything you need?" I asked him.

Grinning, Jericho nodded. "Biscuits. Grand-mère. Sir Richard. You. Yes, I have everything I need."

I chuckled then slid inside. When I closed the door, I caught Richard's reflection in the mirror. "So do I," I whispered softly. "So do I."

Read for the next adventure? Who is Agent Rose? What are Constantine's origins? Find out more about this intriguing pair in *The Society of Roses,* beginning with *Spindles and Thorns.*

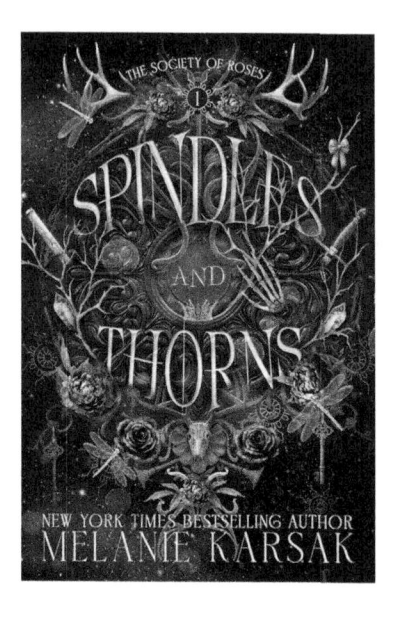

Find this book and more on Amazon

Thank You

I hope you enjoyed Clemeny's adventures. Our beloved Little Red has whispered that she does have a few more stories to tell, but we'll see what the future holds. For now, Clemeny's arc is complete, and her future path is clear. And it's a happy one. I think that's a great place to pause. Thank you for taking this journey with me.

If you enjoyed this novel, would you mind leaving me a review? Reader reviews mean a lot to potential customers, and they help a book become more visible. If you have a moment, I would really appreciate your help.

All my best,
Melanie

Acknowledgments

With special thanks to...

Becky Stephens for helping me shape my words, riding the highs and lows with me, and always being there to pull my ass out of the fire. If it weren't for you, I'd be perpetually covered in hives. Thank you from the bottom of my heart.

Erin Hayes for helping me make my paperbacks beautiful.

Lindsay Galloway for her sharp eyes.

Karri Klawiter for the beautiful covers.

My ARC team for their help with this series.

Lauren Mostura for naming Albertus Stone.

Monica Roman for naming Minuit.

And, as always, to my friends and family for being there to support me. Love you all.

About the Author

New York Times and *USA Today* bestselling author Melanie Karsak is the author of *The Celtic Blood Series, The Road to Valhalla Series, The Celtic Rebels Series, Steampunk Fairy Tales* and many more works of fiction. The author currently lives in Florida with her husband and two children.

- amazon.com/author/melaniekarsak
- facebook.com/authormelaniekarsak
- instagram.com/karsakmelanie
- pinterest.com/melaniekarsak
- bookbub.com/authors/melanie-karsak
- youtube.com/@authormelaniekarsak

Also by Melanie Karsak

THE CELTIC BLOOD SERIES:

Highland Raven

Highland Blood

Highland Vengeance

Highland Queen

THE CELTIC REBELS SERIES:

Queen of Oak: A Novel of Boudica

Queen of Stone: A Novel of Boudica

Queen of Ash and Iron: A Novel of Boudica

THE ROAD TO VALHALLA SERIES:

Under the Strawberry Moon

Shield-Maiden: Under the Howling Moon

Shield-Maiden: Under the Hunter's Moon

Shield-Maiden: Under the Thunder Moon

Shield-Maiden: Under the Blood Moon

Shield-Maiden: Under the Dark Moon

THE SHADOWS OF VALHALLA SERIES:

Shield-Maiden: Winternights Gambit

Shield-Maiden: Gambit of Blood

Shield-Maiden: Gambit of Shadows

Shield-Maiden: Gambit of Swords

Eagles and Crows

The Blackthorn Queen

The Crow Queen

THE HARVESTING SERIES:

The Harvesting

Midway

The Shadow Aspect

Witch Wood

The Torn World

STEAMPUNK FAIRY TALES:

Curiouser and Curiouser: Steampunk Alice in Wonderland

Ice and Embers: Steampunk Snow Queen

Beauty and Beastly: Steampunk Beauty and the Beast

Golden Braids and Dragon Blades: Steampunk Rapunzel

THE RED CAPE SOCIETY

Wolves and Daggers

Alphas and Airships

Peppermint and Pentacles

Bitches and Brawlers

Howls and Hallows

Lycans and Legends

The Airship Racing Chronicles:

Chasing the Star Garden

Chasing the Green Fairy

Chasing Christmas Past

The Chancellor Fairy Tales:

The Glass Mermaid

The Cupcake Witch

The Fairy Godfather

The Vintage Medium

The Book Witch

Find these books and more on Amazon!

Printed in Great Britain
by Amazon